RED SATURDAY

RED SATURDAY

MARTIN ALLEN

faber and faber
LONDON · BOSTON

First published in 1985
by Faber and Faber Limited
3 Queen Square London WC1N 3AU

Set and printed in Great Britain by
Redwood Burn Ltd Trowbridge Wiltshire

British Library Cataloguing in Publication Data

Allen, Martin
Red Saturday.
I. Title
822'.914 PR6051.L539/

ISBN 0-571-13477-7

For Tim Fywell

ACKNOWLEDGEMENTS

For permission to reprint copyright material grateful acknowledgement is made to the following: ATV Music Ltd, 19 Upper Brook Street, London W1Y 1PD, for two lines from 'Don't Sleep in the Subway' by Tony Hatch and Jackie Trent; CBS Songs Ltd, 37 Soho Square, London W1V 5DG for one line from 'Wild Thing' by Chip Taylor © 1965 Blackwood Music Inc. International Copyright secured. All rights reserved; Rondor Music (London) Ltd, Rondor House, 10a, Parsons Green, London SW6 4TW, for one line from 'I Won't Let You Down'.

CHARACTERS

TERRY	aged 19
LEE	aged 31
NOEL	aged 28
DES	in his early forties
FAN	

The play is set in and around present-day Sheffield. The action takes place over a twenty-four-hour period in April.

Red Saturday was first performed at the Gulbenkian Theatre, Canterbury, on 22 October 1983 by the Paines Plough Theatre Company. After a four-week tour the production ran at the New End Theatre, Hampstead, transferring to the Royal Court Theatre Upstairs. The cast was as follows:

TERRY Reece Dinsdale
LEE John Salthouse
NOEL Mark Drewry
DES Eric Richard

Directed by Tim Fywell
Designed by Caroline Beaver

ACT ONE

SCENE ONE

Friday. Early evening.
A modern hotel bedroom with twin beds and a door leading off to a separate bathroom. On one of the beds is an overnight bag.
Sounds off of men passing by outside.
Enter TERRY *dressed casually and carrying an overnight bag and a suit in a suitholder. He puts them on the free bed and looks round the room before hanging the suit in the wardrobe where there is already another suit.*
A loud burst of laughter outside, then LEE, *also dressed casually, opens the door.*

LEE: (*To someone off*) Here! Don't let John the Baptist hear you say that or you'll be out in the wilderness!
(LEE *comes into the room carrying two folders and a carrier bag with a large box inside it.*)
(*Seeing* TERRY) Oh! Am I in the . . .? (*Checks room number.*) Hmm! (*Closes door.*) Terry, isn't it?
TERRY: (*Strong Yorkshire accent*) What? Oh, yeah.
LEE: Must have put us in together. You settling in, then?
TERRY: Yeah. I just found, er, yeah . . .
(LEE *puts the carrier down and throws* TERRY *one of the folders.*)
LEE: Here's your schedule for the weekend. (*Picks up the phone.*) Latest idea from the top. Get you in the right frame o' mind, supposed to. Nice though, aren't they?
TERRY:(*Looking at folder*) Yeah. Smart.
LEE: Names all typed out, responsibilities . . . (*Turns a page.*) Oh, they got who's sharing with who here. Should have looked. (*Feels paper.*) Nice embossment, that . . . (*Into phone*) Room service, please! Two-one-eight. Bottle of Perrier and some ice. Thank you. (*Puts phone down.*) Even got the menus. Look at that! 'Luncheon' page six.
TERRY: Oh aye! 'Soup, boiled fish. . .' What's that for – dinner?
LEE: Yeah. Midday tomorrow before we go to bed. 's lunch, innit? Luncheon!
TERRY: Aw, 'luncheon'! Is that what it means?

LEE: No wonder he wants someone to look after you!

TERRY: We call it 'dinner' in t'middle o' t'day if it's cooked.

LEE: What do you have in the evening then? Elevenses?

TERRY: We call it us 'dinner at teatime'. New to me is that, 'luncheon'. I've heard of 'luncheon meat'.

LEE: Terry, your horizons are about to be broadened. A weekend with me . . . 'Lunch' is what you have in the middle of the day, and what we are about to have is 'dinner'.

TERRY: What's 'supper' then? Says tomorrow, 'Supper will be served on the coach home.'

LEE: Supper . . . 'st another word for 'dinner', innit? For variety. Can't go on saying 'dinner' all the time.

TERRY: There's only one word for breakfast.

LEE: Not such an important meal, is it – breakfast?

TERRY: I don't know! I like a big one most mornings.

LEE: What time do we get back, anyway? Want to get a good night's kip and be out on the links Sunday morning. Do you play?

(LEE *removes a page from the folder and carefully folds it up.*)

TERRY: Haven't for a bit. Used to go two or three times a week wi' our old feller on t'Municipal till I moved down London. Too posh, t'clubs round my way. Don't feel right rolling up in an old Escort with all them Jags and what have you outside. Saab Turbos an' that. (*Beat, as he watches* LEE *pocket the folded page.*) Are you nicking that?

LEE: Be worth hundred quid apiece in twenty years' time, these.

TERRY: Do you reckon?

LEE: Just a bit of research I'm doing – private concern I got on the side. What's your handicap then?

TERRY: I gorrit down to five abaht two year sin'. Dunno what it'd be now.

LEE: I thought I was doing well at nine.

TERRY: I were on t'dole for six months, that's why. Got plenty of practice. Could go round for next to nowt, could t'unemployed. Nowt else to do anyroad.

LEE: (*Starting to unpack.*) What do you do Sundays then if you don't play golf?

TERRY: Stay in bed.

LEE: All day?

TERRY: Till about half eleven. Then I go down t'pub and laik snooker wi' Wayne.

LEE: You want to get some air in your lungs.

TERRY: We walk it off on t'common after.

LEE: You didn't have a preference for any particular bed, did you?

TERRY: No. All t'same to me. Not fucked where I kip.

LEE: Grabbed this one, see? Gives me a good angle on the door case anyone comes in.

TERRY: Who's gonna come in?

LEE: In the night. Never know your luck.

NOEL: (*Off*) Room service!

LEE: Come in!

(*Enter* NOEL *in a suit and tie, arm in a sling, carrying a tray of Perrier water and ice, a waiter's napkin over his free arm.*)

Oh, no!

NOEL: Your drinks, sir.

LEE: You tosser! I was expecting that little blonde piece.

NOEL: I saw her off for you, Lee. Can't have you being distracted on a night like tonight.

LEE: Not sure I should let you in actually with that arm. It's not catching, is it?

NOEL: I shouldn't think so. Here – have a butcher's!

LEE: Leave it out, Noel! Got problems of my own without you!

NOEL: You'll be all right.

LEE: Not with you, I won't. Who's he put you in with, then?

NOEL: Magnus Magnusson.

LEE: You're joking! 'I've started so I'll finish'?

NOEL: I've just left him unpacking.

LEE: Not brought all them books again, has he? Be up all night putting shelves up if he has.

NOEL: I saw a couple of guides to Sheffield and the Peaks.

LEE: Wonder he hasn't packed his climbing boots. Anyway, he don't need a guidebook with that wrist-watch he has. Have you seen it? Like a ship's chronometer. Surprised he wasn't up at the front of the coach navigating for Arthur.

NOEL: What's he split us up for, then?

LEE: You're in quarantine, mate. Keep telling you. I don't want to pick up anything nasty.

NOEL: No, seriously.

LEE: I suppose it's so me and Terry here can develop a good working relationship for the weekend. Show him the ropes, get him psyched up proper and so on.

NOEL: How you feeling, Tel? Nervous?

TERRY: Bit.

LEE: Don't worry! You'll be terrified tomorrow.

TERRY: (*To* NOEL) Have I taken your bed?

NOEL: Nah! No sweat! He's always chopping and changing us.

(TERRY *starts to unpack. He has one or two comics in his bag which he hides from the others.*)

LEE: (*To* NOEL) You're lucky to be here anyway with that.

NOEL: Didn't want me to feel left out.

LEE: That what he said?

NOEL: Didn't want a sense of isolation to creep in.

LEE: Big of him.

NOEL: He has some very funny ways you know, Terry. Do you think you'll be all right?

TERRY: I can look after missen.

NOEL: You want to make a reservation for the bathroom before dinner for a start. He has to do his hair.

LEE: Hark who's talking! I hope you've told Sherpa Tensing through there he can't have a bath after nine-thirty.

NOEL: Oh, I'm going to be soaking myself with this, aren't I? Had to get Paula to scrub me down last night. Felt a right prat.

LEE: (*To* TERRY) It's all down to years sharing with him I have to wash it before dinner anyway. Can't get a look-in afterwards.

NOEL: Well, now I'm not here you can take your pick, can't you?

LEE: That's true. You thinking of taking a shower or anything, Terry?

TERRY: Nah. I might give my face, neck and arms a quick wesh.

LEE: Spoilt for choice.

NOEL: Well, don't have a brain tumour worrying about it, will you? I best get back, anyway. Just popped in to get my bearings.

LEE: Yeah, all right, Noel.

NOEL: I'll see you at dinner.

LEE: Unless he's got place names out for us.

NOEL: (*Picking up folder*) Yeah. What do you think of 'em?

LEE: Bit naff, aren't they?

NOEL: Must have cost a few quid.
LEE: Be wearing name badges next.
NOEL: (*Reads*:) 'Morning perambulation will commence at ten-thirty. Personnel are asked to check in promptly at the departure area.'
LEE: What's he doing? Launching a fucking rocket? We're only going for a walk!
NOEL: I'm off, anyway.
LEE: OK. See you later, pal. Don't do anything I'd do.
NOEL: See you, Terry!
TERRY: Yeah. Tara!
(*Exit* NOEL.)
LEE: Thank God he's gone!
TERRY: Why?
LEE: I don't know what Dawesy's playing about at, bringing him up here.
TERRY: What's up with him?
LEE: Didn't you see?
TERRY: What? His arm?
LEE: There was a bloke in America once had arm like that. He kept feeling this itching under the plaster. Then when they took it off they found ants had got underneath it and burrowed down into his bone.
TERRY: Honest?
LEE: Eaten all the marrow away.
TERRY: (*Beat.*) I think I will have a wash if it's all right, Lee.
LEE: Yeah, yeah. You go ahead. Anything you need, just sing out! It's what I'm here for.
TERRY: (*Putting his shoes on the table*) I think I've got everything . . .
LEE: Watch what you're doing, Terry!
TERRY: Eh?
LEE: On the table! Your shoes!
TERRY: It's all right. They're clean.
LEE: (*Moving to swipe them off*) Take the fuckers. . . !
(TERRY *removes them, astonished at the outburst.*)
Not in the hotel, Terry! Night before the big day!
TERRY: (*Putting them on the floor*) Sorry.
LEE: Bloody hell!
(TERRY *goes into the bathroom.* LEE *picks up the phone.*)
Outside line please, love. Two-one-eight. Ta. (*Dials,*

inspecting a bottle of Terry's deodorant as he does so.) Hello, Eric? Lee. I'm in Sheffield. Any news? Course there's one hour's difference over there, isn't there? In front or behind, I can never remember. Listen, I been thinking. What I'd like to do is go over some time for a day or two and see it for myself. You reckon you could fix it? I mean, it's a big move. I'm still interested, yeah. It's a question of that, and how much money they can come up with, like we were saying. Yeah, all right. It's Sheffield 665696. Try about ten, ten-thirty, OK? Thanks, Eric. Tara! (*Depresses the hook briefly.*) Another outside line please, love. Lee Merter, that's right. Is that . . .? I thought I recognized that voice. Wilma, isn't it? That place out on the moors? Oh, not so bad. How's yourself? What you doing down here, then? More money? I won't be short of a bob or two after tomorrow with any luck, I can tell you. We'll be down later on. You can buy me an orange juice. Yeah, all right, darling! That's it. See you later, then. Tara!
(LEE *dials again. As he does so,* TERRY *strolls on briefly, brushing his teeth vigorously. He nods casually to* LEE *before going back into the bathroom.*)
Oh, hello there. Yeah. About half-hour ago. No news, no. I've just rung him. How are you – all right? How's Warren? Rebecca all right? And you're OK? I know I saw you this morning! Just thought I'd ask. No! No, well actually, the reason I'm ringing, love, is the dog. Oh, don't start, Steph! We agreed all this when we bought him. Course I'd have rung you anyway! You wasn't saying that at Walthamstow two weeks back when he won the silver collar and you had your picture in the *Gazette*. Anyway, let's not start, eh? You know I got a big day tomorrow. (*Feels his right foot.*) Seems to have got worse. Must have knocked it out on the way up. He's gonna go bananas when I tell him. Look, what about the dog, anyway? I just think you should take him round to Don's in the morning, that's all. Let him have a look at that ear. Well, after you've taken Warren to the doctor, then! Not gonna be there all morning, are you? He'll go in the back of the Audi. You know I'd do it myself if . . . All right – when? I can't, Tuesday. I'm seeing Oliver about that red demand. You know – the tax. I'll do it Thursday. Yeah, promise. Cos I'll

have time in the morning to get the paint. Good. All right then . . . Yeah. Thanks. Oh, and, love?, don't forget his calcium tablets, will you? Only Don says they're good for his gums. All right, then. Tara! (*Puts phone down and reaches for the Perrier.*) Things I do for that dog!

(LEE *drinks, gets up, and walks round the room, anxiously testing his weight on his right foot. Then he opens his toilet bag and selects a number of bottles. Re-enter* TERRY, *rubbing himself down.*)

TERRY: Right. That's me finished.

LEE: That was quick!

TERRY: Is it all right to use that phone?

LEE: Who you ringing? A speech therapist? (*Beat.*) You have to be 21.

TERRY: Do you have to pay?

LEE: Nah. All goes on the account.

TERRY: (*Using his deodorant*) Might ring mi mam.

LEE: I was wondering what that was for. I mean, it's only April. Still a bit cold for flies, isn't it?

(*Beat, as* LEE *sees* TERRY *is hurt.*)

My bit o' fun, Tel. Seriously, though, you want to get something decent. Here! (*Throws his own deodorant to* TERRY.) Take a sniff o' that!

TERRY: (*Smelling it*) Can hardly smell owt!

LEE: Course you can't! Don't want to leave trails of it behind you, do you?

TERRY: (*Returning it*) What's in that box?

LEE: What? Oh, open it if you like.

(TERRY *opens the box inside the carrier to find a new football.*)

TERRY: Oh, nice one! Who's it for?

LEE: Max Towner gave me it on the way up. Wants us all to sign it.

TERRY: (*Playing with the ball*) Were that that bloke in t'blue cardigan having tea with us?

LEE: That's him.

TERRY: Who's he when he's at home, then?

LEE: Max? One of the fans. Don't let him hear you talking like that!

TERRY: Must be keen, coming all t'way up here to watch us have tea.

LEE: Missed two games in the last fifteen years.

TERRY: Chuff me! Where's he get his money from?
LEE: He's a butcher.
TERRY: Is that 'Towner's' who has t'adverts on Capital Radio?
LEE: That's it. Worth a fortune, that feller. It's for his godson or something. (*Going to bathroom*) Needs a special pen though.
TERRY: Can you just show us how to use that phone?
LEE: Well, Terry. You lift the receiver, yeah? And you'll hear a little lady's voice saying, 'Hello? Can I help you?' And you say, 'Outside line, please . . .'
TERRY: OK, OK . . .
(*A flicker of tension.*)
LEE: Yeah?
TERRY: Let's see . . . What time is it? Mi mam'll be at t'club. (*Lifts the receiver.*)
LEE: (*Going into bathroom*) Course, you're from round here, ain't you?
TERRY: Used to have a paper round along this road.
LEE: (*Off*) No, really?
TERRY: Yeah.
LEE: (*Off*) You should have said.
TERRY: (*Into phone*) Er, can I have an outside line please? (*Dials.*) I were allus glad when I'd dropped off here cos it made my bag a lot lighter. Eight or nine papers a day they used to get. Posh stuff, you know – *Yorkshire Post* an' that. Used to cadge cigs off t'bloke 'at used to wash t'steps.
LEE: (*Off*) Tables turned now, eh?
TERRY: Aye. Takes a bit o' getting used to.
LEE: (*Off*) They still live round here, your old folks?
TERRY: Live near. Knocked all . . . (*Into phone*) Hello? Is that the Metropolitan? Can I speak to Mrs Bishop, please? She waits on in the Stork Room. Thank you very much. (*Beat.*) Mam? It's Terry. Yeah. I've got here. 'baht forty minutes sin'. Eh, guess where we're staying! In t'Cumberland! Oh, it's dead posh. Bed apiece, private bathroom, phone for you to use an' t'club pays. I'm on t'phone now. I can't. We've to stay in t'hotel to get you in t'right attitude. Did you get them tickets, anyroad? They're seats, tha knows. You're not standing. We'll be at Wembley next month if we win tomorrow. On t'telly live. Oh, ask mi dad! He'll explain it. Is he? Yeah, all right. Thanks. Yeah. Tara then! (*Beat.*)

Hello? I'm all reet. In t'Cumberland – I were telling mi mam. Eh! Guess who I'm sharing a room wi'! Lee Merter. Honest. Noel Cooper's got a broken arm still an' it were between me an' Wayne Adams and I got it.
(LEE, *a towel round his head, appears at the bathroom door.*) Midfield. On t'left, so it's my best side. Oh, don't feel so bad. Bit nervous, tha knows. What you doin' down at t'club, anyroad? Bit early for you, int it? (*Laughs.*) Tea room? I dunno. What's it say on t'ticket? Does it? Oh, you needn't bother, Dad. No. Oh, all right then. If you want. I better go, anyway. We're going down for dinner in a minute. Yeah. I'll give you a wave. All right. Thanks. Tara then! Tara! (*Puts the phone down.*)

LEE: You better not score any goals tomorrow.

TERRY: What for?

LEE: 'Tha knows'!

TERRY: It's Yorkshire.

LEE: Talking to Barry Davies and coming out with mouthfuls like that! He'll think he's talking to that Polish bloke who plays for them. (*Going back into the bathroom*) How comes you're with a London club if you're from up here, anyway?

TERRY: (*Starting to dress for dinner*) Scout from QPR saw us at a youth game. He couldn't use me but he passed word on to Mr Dawes. Next thing I knew I were down London having trials.

LEE: (*Off*) And he signed you up?

TERRY: Not straight off. Couldn't make his mind up.

LEE: (*Off*) Typical!

TERRY: I had trials wi' Wednesday an' United an' all when I were laikin' for t'City boys. Dad told me to hold out for a First Division club though.

LEE: (*Off*) Sounds like a shrewd feller.

TERRY: If it ant a been for him . . .

LEE: (*Off*) Fan o' mine, is he?

TERRY: Sort of.

LEE: (*Off*) What's he do?

TERRY: Fitter at t'power station.

LEE: (*Off*) What's he fit?

TERRY: Oh, you know. Parts an' that. (*Beat.*) First game he ever took me to were to see you.

LEE: (*Off*) When was that?

TERRY: Seventy-one. Quarter-final.

LEE: (*Off*) At Leeds?

TERRY: He kept saying, 'Watch out for number ten – Merter. One o' t'best inside forwards in England. Watch how he keeps losing his marker.' Dint know what he were on about first. Thought it were somat you kept in your pocket that you had to keep dropping. Then, when you got that second goal I saw what he meant.

LEE: (*Coming back on, rubbing his hair with a towel*) Do you remember that?

TERRY: Went round three defenders just outside t'box an' knocked it in from twenty yards. Goalie dived into t'post trying to save it.

LEE: How old was you?

TERRY: Seven an' half.

LEE: Now here you are . . . It's like George Wells, the old manager, used to say. 'Football, gentlemen, is the ladder to the stars for the sons of the people.' Great man, George. (*Starts brushing his hair.*) Suppose it started you off, did it, seeing me pull that brace?

TERRY: Oh no! I knew already.

LEE: What? Before you was seven?

TERRY: Known as long as I can remember. Used to be out every night on t'streets, laikin' wi' mi mates till they'd all been called in. Then when I were on my own I'd spend another half-hour practising mi skills.

LEE: When was you born then?

TERRY: 1964. Year West Ham beat Preston North End three–two at Wembley.

LEE: Did you see that, an' all?

TERRY: Holden after nine minutes for Preston; Sissons equalized a minute later; Dawson after forty minutes; two–one to Preston at half-time. Hurst after fifty-two minutes for West Ham equalized; and Ronnie Boyce got t'winner two minutes into injury . . .

LEE: All right, all right! Getting ready for a football match, not *Criss Cross Quiz*! That'd be more use, if you could tell me the team for tomorrow! (*Aggressively getting his hairdryer together*) Won't see my kids hanging about on street corners till all hours, getting into mischief. In bed by half-past seven at that age . . . (*Looks round bedroom walls.*) Where's the sockets in this place?

TERRY: Aren't they by t'bed?

LEE: Dunno why I'm bothering, anyway. Not gonna be playing with this ankle.

TERRY: You were telling Des it were all right at teatime.

LEE: Cos he's such a worrier, that's why! (*Finding sockets*) Look where they've put 'em! (*Throws hairdryer on bed.*) How do they expect me to reach down there? What a poxy dump!

TERRY: What's up with it?

LEE: Nothing up with it if you don't mind carrying hundred yards of electric cable round with you every time you want to dry your hair. (*Starts to dress.*) Never used to come here when George was in charge. Took us out on the moors, somewhere smart. Bit o' refinement. Decent mirrors for a start. Not them spastic things in that apology for a bathroom!

TERRY: (*Indignant*) It's one o' t'best hotels in Sheffield, t'Cumberland.

LEE: Part of a chain, I expect. You pay to look into mirrors like that down the seafront at Brighton. Same that time in Helsinki once. Over the bed they were. Ended up dreaming I was a midget. Got beat by a team of amateurs the next day. Worked in a rubber-johnny factory if I remember right. Pissed on 'em in the second leg, no problem, but still . . . (*Looking into mirror*) Oh, no!

TERRY: What?

LEE: I got a blackhead coming an' all now! You got any Germolene or anything?

TERRY: Put some soap on it.

LEE: Soap! That's where I miss Noel. Regular as clockwork with the embrocations, him. Don't want that thing on the screen tomorrow if there's any close-ups.

TERRY: They won't want to talk to me, will they? On t'telly?

LEE: (*Resuming dressing*) They might do. Get to Wembley and they'll want to know everything about you. Haven't you filled that questionnaire in yet?

TERRY: What questionnaire?

LEE: In the folder.

TERRY: (*Getting the folder*) I didn't know there wa one.

LEE: Asks you all sorts of things. Kind o' music you like, where you go for your holidays . . .

TERRY: Reighton Gap we went last . . .
LEE: Sexual preferences . . .
TERRY: Sex? (*Still looking in folder*) I can't seem to fin' this thing.
LEE: Near the end it should be.
TERRY: They don't want to know about us love lives, do they?
LEE: Wanted to know what your ambitions are, if I remember.
TERRY: Oh easy! Regular first-team player for t'club. I reckon I could be one o' t'best four in t'team if I work at it.
LEE: Oh, yeah? Who's the other three then?
TERRY: (*Counting on fingers*) Me, Lloyd . . .
LEE: Yeah?
TERRY: Me, Lloyd . . . Baptiste . . . I'm talking about three or four years' time.
LEE: Yeah, well, go on!
TERRY: I mean, if you want my top four now . . .
LEE: No, go on! Four years' time.
TERRY: It's hard cos you don't know who'll still be here.
LEE: Well, if there's no changes.
TERRY: Then again, you don't know how people'll turn out. Top four now'd be you, Lloyd . . .
LEE: Not interested in it now! It's four years' time we're talking about. Come on! Who'll it be? You, Lloyd, Baptiste, and . . . ?
TERRY: Depend.
LEE: Yeah? What on?
TERRY: (*Shrugs.*) Who comes up.
LEE: All right, Russell Grant! Who's gonna come up?
TERRY: (*Returning to folder*) Where do you say it wa? Near t'end?
LEE: Perhaps just regular players they've given one to, Terry. (*There is a knock at the door, and without waiting for a reply,* DES, *wearing a suit and tie, comes in, closing the door behind him.*)
Hello! Trouble!
DES: All right, lads?
LEE: What you doing in here?
DES: (*To* LEE) You want to look sharp! It's nearly half-past. You been gassing again?
LEE: I been helping him get settled in.
DES: How you feeling, Terry? All right?

TERRY: Yeah.

DES: Not giving you a hard time, is he?

TERRY: Nah.

DES: Good, good. That's it – put your suit on for dinner. Is that tie fastened properly?

TERRY: Dunno.

DES: Let's have a look.

(DES *adjusts* TERRY'*s tie and helps him on with his jacket, while* LEE *continues to dress alone, watching the others.*)

And keep it on tonight. Got to look smart when we're all together in public. On show, remember. Outsiders in here tonight'll judge the club for the rest of their lives on what they see this evening. Don't want 'em thinking we're a bunch of hooligans in jeans and bomber jackets, do we? Shouting and screaming . . .

LEE: Do you think I'll need my woolly vest on, Des?

DES: (*To* TERRY) Comedian. Your mum an' dad gonna be there tomorrow?

TERRY: Yeah.

DES: How are they? All right?

TERRY: Yes, thank you very much.

DES: Dad still make his own beer?

TERRY: Makes wine an' all now.

DES: Seems a long time now since I used to have to come up here to fetch you back down, doesn't it? Eh? Every other week at one stage, if I remember.

LEE: Is that when you learnt to speak the language, Des?

DES: Wouldn't have dared bring you up here two years ago in case you ran off.

LEE: Now here he is on his cup début.

TERRY: I feel a bit sorry for Wayne though, not getting it.

DES: We'll put him back in if you're feeling cut up about it, Terry.

(TERRY *doesn't answer.*)

You worry about your own game. Never mind about him! (*Finishes adjusting the tie.*) There you are! That's better!

LEE: My turn now, is it?

DES: You'll be lucky! (*Beat.*) Did you ring that feller back, by the way?

LEE: Which feller?

DES: From Barcelona.

LEE: Barcelona?

DES: Didn't Julie tell you? Rang Thursday morning. Wanted to know when your contract runs out. Next year, isn't it?

LEE: Next year, yeah. But what did he want?

DES: She couldn't understand what he was saying – you know, jabbering on in broken English like they do – so she put the phone down.

LEE: She did what?

DES: I told her you wouldn't be too pleased.

LEE: And when you say this was? Yesterday?

DES: Sounded quite excited as well by all accounts. Yesterday, yeah. I think she said Barcelona. Began with a B.

LEE: Not Bruges?

DES: No. Barcelona. (*Beat.*) Or was it Brentford?

LEE: You bleeder!

DES: Come on, Lee! Not trying to get rid of you just yet. Thirty-one not 41.

LEE: Yeah. Your privilege, that.

DES: Year or two's time and we might start thinking about bringing in a new striker. (*Beat.*) What's all this about Bruges, anyway?

LEE: (*Dismissive, as he resumes dressing*) Oh . . . something in the paper. You know. Rumour . . .

DES: Not thinking of leaving us, are you?

LEE: Don't worry! Don't get rid of me that easy.

(DES *looks at* LEE *briefly but doesn't pursue it.*)

DES: You hungry, Terry?

TERRY: Could eat horse.

DES: Get a big dinner inside you. Plenty of carbohydrates. Lee'll show you. Potatoes, steak-and-kidney pudding . . . It's your fuel. It'll turn into energy tomorrow. And there's jam roly-poly with custard for sweet.

LEE: We have been perusing the à la carte actually, Des.

DES: It's Graham's idea, that. Says it gives the weekend a unity.

LEE: Learn it on that management course he went on, did he?

DES: If he thinks it's gonna help our attitude . . . You have to try these things. And plenty of sleep tonight, Terry.

TERRY: Early night?

DES: As long as you get eight or nine hours. Breakfast in bed if you want it. Apart from that, just relax. (*Beat.*) Nothing new anyway about getting a big dinner night before a match. Should have seen the dumplings we used to have to put away. Like snooker balls, some of 'em.

LEE: (*To* TERRY) You wouldn't think he used to be able to run around for ninety minutes, would you, looking at him? Them long baggy shorts they used to wear. Big hobnail boots . . .

DES: I'd give you ten yards start any day.

VOICE: (*Off*) Dinner in five minutes!

DES: Hurry up, Lee! Not Player of the Year Award Dinner! I told you I wanted him down in that dining room by seven-thirty sharp!

LEE: Gift-wrapped or as he is?

DES: I only hope your feet work as hard as your mouth tomorrow afternoon. Thrash 'em fifteen–nil if they do. Come on anyway, Terry! (*Leading him off*) Take you down myself. No point waiting . . .

LEE: Oh, Des! Before you go . . .

DES: What?

LEE: I meant to tell you something.

(*Pause as* LEE *says nothing.*)

DES: Go on, then!

LEE: I think I might have put my foot out again.

DES: You what?

LEE: I think I felt it go on the coach up.

DES: You're joking!

LEE: I'm not, no.

DES: (*Coming back in*) Are you sure?

LEE: I'm fairly sure. I mean . . .

DES: (*Getting down to it*) Why didn't you tell me?

LEE: I wasn't sure if I was imagining it, but . . .

DES: Where can you feel it? Here?

LEE: (*Enjoying the attention*) . . . don't seem to be getting any better. Just there, yeah.

DES: Only here?

LEE: Well, sort of all over . . .

DES: It's not hurting you here, is it? Just here, when I squeeze?

LEE: It is, yeah.

DES: Blood and snot! (*Gets up.*) Sounds like you've done that ligament again. Why didn't you tell me at teatime?

LEE: I didn't want to worry you if it wasn't . . .

DES: Who do you think you are? Captain Oates? There's no

place for heroics in this operation, Lee! Join the army if it's decorations you want! We're in the winning business here. Team effort. Fitness. I don't care if it's a broken neck or a morning-after headache. I want to know about it! Understand?

LEE: Yeah, I know . . .

DES: You bloody well should know an' all! Your experience! I put you in here to set the lad an example. Not teach him this bloody rubbish! Straightaway, I want to know! Straightaway! (*Pause.*) Anyway, nothing we can do about it tonight. Have to kick a ball at you tomorrow morning and see . . .

LEE: Yeah, well don't kick it too hard, will you? Injuries have a nasty habit of suddenly getting worse in these last-minute fitness tests. Know what I mean? Specially when people like Wayne are travelling.

DES: Sod Wayne! It's you we want! Tch! Thought we'd sorted it out, that foot. Just go steady on it tonight. OK?

LEE: Yeah, OK.

DES: Have to keep our fingers crossed. (*To* TERRY) You see now why I put you in here! How not to relax, night before a cup tie. He hasn't been talking to you about it, has he?

TERRY: What? His foot?

DES: (*To* LEE) Just thank your lucky stars I'm not Graham Dawes! You'd have known about it then, I can tell you. (*To himself*) Bloody hell! I don't know . . .

(DES *leads* TERRY *off.* LEE *stays behind briefly to have a last look in the mirror.*)

(*Off*) Do you think you'll be down for breakfast, Lee?

(*Exit* LEE, *carrying his right foot slightly.*)

SCENE TWO

The same, later that evening.
Enter LEE, *who stands at the door talking to* NOEL *off.*

NOEL: (*Off*) Get a good night then, won't you?
LEE: Aren't you coming in?
NOEL: (*Off*) I want to ring Paula . . .
LEE: (*Dragging* NOEL *in*) Come on! It's only quarter-past ten! Sit yourself down!
(NOEL, *who is carrying a newspaper, sits down.*)
(*Closing the door*) Drink?
NOEL: Yeah, OK.
LEE: (*Picking up phone*) What you want? Scotch? Rémy?
NOEL: Leave it out, Lee! You got that Perrier, haven't you?
LEE: You can have a sharpener! Not playing tomorrow.
NOEL: No, but you are!
LEE: Don't make me laugh! With this foot? That's why he's brought Wayne up, to go in for me. Gonna need a drink anyway with all that racket going on downstairs from that Rotary Club do. Won't be able to sleep otherwise.
NOEL: No alcohol for me though, Lee. And you ought to go careful.
LEE: Not going to get anything at this rate. Suppose they're at full stretch pandering to those moneybags. (*Into phone*) Hello? Can I speak to Wilma, please? Room two-one-eight. She'll know who it is. (*To* NOEL) You remember Wilma? That place up on the moors?
NOEL: Oh, yeah! Her you got to know that time?
(LEE *nods.*)
What's she doing down here?
LEE: Booked in for the weekend when she heard we were coming. Thought we might get her up here later on. Get rid of Terry. You remember the tricks we used to get up to in the old days?
NOEL: That was years ago.
LEE: Never too young. (*Into phone*) Hello, Wilma? Oh, has she? Oh. When's she coming back? I see. You leave her a message? Tell her I called and, er, say I was just wondering

how room service compared in the two hotels. She'll know what I mean. OK. Thanks a lot. (*Puts phone down.*) She's supervising something at that dinner dance. Be up later. You want a Perrier then?

NOEL: Yeah, I'll have a small one.

(LEE *pours them both a drink.*)

LEE: (*Giving* NOEL *the drink*) Here you are.

NOEL: Cheers!

LEE: You all right?

NOEL: Yeah! No, it's just when I was going into the games room I could have sworn I saw Eddie.

LEE: Eddie Sellers?

NOEL: Yeah. Wasn't him of course, but just for a minute . . .

LEE: He'll be in Edmonton Friday night, counting up the shekels. How's his demolition business?

NOEL: Collapsed. Haven't you heard? I saw him a couple of weeks back getting off the bus with his two kids. Stooped shoulders, losing his hair . . . Works in a biscuit factory now, he was telling me, making tea. Wife earns more than him. Typist at a travel agent's.

LEE: (*Unconcerned*) No kidding?

NOEL: I remember him in the showers once after training, asking me if I'd buy him a ticket for the big matches in a few years' time. I thought he was winding me up cos I was only about 19, and there he was, Scottish international and everything . . . He never mentioned it again but it reminded me the other week, seeing him in his old anorak, buying programmes for his kids, going out on to the terraces incognito . . .

LEE: Well, if you blow all your money without planning it . . . They'll get free holidays if she works in a travel agent's, won't they?

NOEL: Suppose they will, yeah.

LEE: (*Holding his stomach*) Bloody dinner! Be having nightmares, all them carbohydrates he makes us eat.

NOEL: He doesn't usually play midfield, does he?

LEE: Terry? Plays all over in the reserves. Why? You getting worried?

NOEL: About what?

LEE: In case he has a good game?

NOEL: I thought he was a striker?

LEE: He'll play wherever he can get a foothold, young lad like him.

NOEL: Better watch out yourself then, hadn't you?

LEE: No chance! Mind you, if that Barcelona deal comes off . . .

NOEL: What Barcelona deal?

LEE: Their chairman rang the club yesterday morning, asking about my availability.

NOEL: Straight up?

LEE: Ringing him back Monday. See what he's offering. There's a club with money.

NOEL: They just bought a new striker, haven't they? That Argentine?

LEE: One of their scouts been watching me, according to Des. And Bruges. Name's been connected with them apparently. Not the same class as Barcelona, of course, but they got some good players now, the Belgiums.

NOEL: Oh, I know. No disgrace to play there any more.

LEE: Some good restaurants in Brussels by all accounts. And you're only half-hour from Heathrow.

NOEL: You thinking about it, then?

LEE: They've got to make a formal approach yet. (*Beat.*) Time for a change anyway, now that new twat's in charge.

NOEL: You reckon?

LEE: I mean, how can you work with a man who sits up in the directors' box and phones his instructions down? He should be out on the bench screaming his head off at us. Not been the same since George left. Got no emotions, this new geezer. Seems to brood . . .

NOEL: He's just a bit quiet.

LEE: You see him tonight wandering around with his dinky little schedules under his arm? Scowling and scratching his bum? Like a roaming rectum. (*Beat.*) And look at this place he brings us to!

NOEL: You're right there. I been looking at the finishing.

LEE: You imagine George bringing us here? For a semi-final? Paper serviettes and one portion of butter each? (*Sees* NOEL *has finished his drink.*) More Perrier?

NOEL: No, I'm all right. I best push in a minute. Catch a bit of the darts.

LEE: (*Going to television set*) You can watch it in here. What station's it on?

NOEL: No, don't bother, Lee. I wouldn't be watching it, only it's Keith Deller. He's a mate of our Steve's. Must fix up with Steve actually about the summer.

LEE: Going to Jersey again?

NOEL: Helping him put his central heating in.

LEE: On your holidays?

NOEL: Learn how to do it from him then I can put my own in. Save about a thousand quid doing it that way.

LEE: You must have been working on that house ever since I've known you.

NOEL: Move in next summer with any luck. I used to be apprentice joiner, don't forget, before I turned pro.

LEE: You might have to go back to it if Dawesy puts Plan X into operation.

NOEL: (*Beat.*) It's been making me think, though, this arm. You know – out of action, standing on the terraces watching all the other lads train . . . You realize you're not so important as you thought you were. New faces coming in. People like Terry wearing your shirt . . . Doing a good job as well.

LEE: Don't take me the wrong way, Noel . . .

NOEL: No, no . . .

LEE: I mean, you're only 27.

NOEL: Twenty-eight! Stands to reason Graham'll want to forge his own identity on the club. Been here for three years now. Not gonna want to live in George's shadow forever.

LEE: He's not going to dismantle a winning team. Just like that. Might shake it up a bit, but . . .

NOEL: George's team, Lee. Dismantle itself in a year or two's time.

LEE: Not the stalwarts like you though, Noel! You've no need to start making plans. I'm only talking about myself when . . .

NOEL: No, but we all got to think about it. I'm already half a yard down on last season . . .

LEE: There's no need to get morbid!

NOEL: I'm not getting morbid. It's a question of planning, isn't it?

LEE: Well, like you say, you got your bricks to fall back on.

NOEL: I was talking to Paula's cousin the other night. He was on at me to do what he's doing.

LEE: What's that?
NOEL: Police.
LEE: Oof! Jesus!
NOEL: Said he'd bring some brochures round one evening.
LEE: Do anything, won't they, some people?
NOEL: Well, secure job, decent money... Been doing a lot for the force, this Government.
LEE: You being serious?
NOEL: Somebody's got to do it. Need a police force.
LEE: You need referees and linesmen too, but it's the blokes who go in for it.
NOEL: He seems a nice enough chap – Kevin.
LEE: You'll get the odd fart that don't smell, yeah, but... the Old Bill, Noel! After playing in the First Division!
NOEL: Well, what you gonna do?
LEE: We're there to excite the crowds, not control them!
NOEL: We're not gonna be exciting anybody in ten years' time, Lee.
LEE: Long way off yet.
NOEL: What are you gonna do?
LEE: (*Picking up the ball*) I got plenty of ideas. Want to try my hand at PR for a start. You know, Harry Swales kind of thing. Agent for sports personalities. Office in Bond Street. 'Lee Merter Enterprises'. Travel all over the world doing that. Keep on the move. That's the important thing.
(LEE *starts to play with the ball.*)
NOEL: (*Watching him*) I thought you had a bad foot?
LEE: I have. Still pretty sharp though, aren't I? On the old ball control? (*Does a fancy trick.*) How about that?
NOEL: (*Opening his paper to a page he has evidently already read*) 'Merter's flashes of brilliance in set pieces make him lethal in the box.'
LEE: There you are, you see!
NOEL: (*Still reading*:) 'Hillsborough will hold its breath in anticipation when he walks on centre stage...'
LEE: (*Stops playing.*) Come on, Noel! Let's go down to that ballroom and have a game o' shots-in. Give them blue-rinsed old bastards the fright o' their lives! How about it? Nobody'll know.
NOEL: (*Folding paper up*) Too risky.

LEE: You miserable bugger! I bring you in here for a bit of a laugh . . .

NOEL: (*Getting up*) It's getting on, anyway. I'm going to bed early these days. Want to get fit and playing again as quick as I can.

LEE: Wilma'll be up in ten minutes.

NOEL: You can have her all to yourself, then.

LEE: I won't be able to manage. You know what she's like.

NOEL: No, I don't.

LEE: Go on, then! (*Opening door and pushing* NOEL *out*) Piss off! Prophet o' doom!

NOEL: Sleep well, Lee.

LEE: Here! Leave me the paper, at least!

(NOEL *gives him it.*)

And don't forget to lock your door!

NOEL: Why?

LEE: Don't want any visitors in the night, do you? White-faced man in old anorak, pair o' boots round his neck, rifling your wallet for tickets.

NOEL: Fuck off!

(LEE *laughs, and* NOEL *exits.* LEE *eagerly starts searching in the paper for the report* NOEL *was reading from. A knock on the door makes him look up in panic.*)

LEE: (*Finally*) Hello?

(*Enter* TERRY.)

Oh, bloody hell!

TERRY: 's up?

LEE: (*Taking his jacket off and sitting down*) Nothing, Terry. Nothing. Come in! Sit down! Make yourself at home!

(TERRY *sits down and* LEE *gets out a notebook and pen.*)

Are you going to go through life knocking on every door you come to?

TERRY: Dunno. (*Beat.*) All t'other lads have gone in to watch Keith Deller.

LEE: (*Writing*) Who?

TERRY: You know Keith Deller! That darts player. Not much older than me an' he's already one o' t'best in t'world.

LEE: Never heard of him.

TERRY: He's on now. We could watch him together if you put t'telly on.

LEE: I happen to be busy, Terry. Anyway, I never watch telly night before a game. Makes my ears sing.

TERRY: (*Beat.*) What you writing?
LEE: Just a few notes. Go in round about chapter seven, this bit.
TERRY: Is it a book?
LEE: Autobiography.
TERRY: Honest?
LEE: Publisher's been on at me to let him have a copy. Keep telling him you can't just knock these things off.
TERRY: What you gonna call it?
LEE: *Lee of the Storm*.
TERRY: Smart! (*Beat.*) I just won three quid at cards.
LEE: Must have been a comedown from Curzon Street.
TERRY: I'm surprised you don't belong to a card school, Lee.
LEE: Are you?
TERRY: Passes t'time on, takes your mind off t'game.
LEE: Keep it up a couple o' years and you won't have a mind to take off.
TERRY: What you been doing, then?
LEE: Oh, this an' that. Did my rounds after dinner. Had ten minutes with Max. Here – you can sign his ball. (*Closes his notebook and gives the ball and pen to* TERRY.) Bumped into the hotel manager. Picked his brains on the catering business up here. Had a look at the register. They got that bloke from *Celebrity Squares* staying.
TERRY: (*Laboriously signing the ball*) Honest?
LEE: Up on the sixth floor, away from the noise. Makes sure he gets the VIP treatment.
TERRY: Must be doing a turn at one o' t'clubs.
LEE: Finished up in the snooker room with Ian, practising my aiming skills.
TERRY: I were trying to get on them tables but Mr Dawes came in for me.
LEE: Stop calling him 'Mr Dawes', for God's sake! Anybody'd think he was a human being. (*Beat.*) What did he want, anyway?
TERRY: See how I felt an' that. Took me into t'bar to meet a director. Raymond Standup or somat.
LEE: Standish?
TERRY: Oh, aye, that were it.
LEE: What's he poking his snout in for?
TERRY: Kept asking me questions. Then when I were answering he kept looking at them waitresses in t'black

stockings taking drinks through to that dinner dance.

LEE: Set a wonderful example, don't they? Still, I suppose it was more interesting for him. (*Looks at* TERRY *still signing the ball.*) You can just put a little cross on if it's easier and I'll write your name underneath.

TERRY: You're reet. I've nearly finished. There!

(TERRY *starts to play with the ball impressively.*)

LEE: Oh, nice one!

(TERRY *flicks it over to* LEE. *There is a sequence of passes till* LEE *opts out by catching it.*)

Don't want to make that foot worse than it is. Not that I'll be playing of course . . .

TERRY: Is it no better?

LEE: Waste o' time me coming up here.

TERRY: (*Not pursuing it*) Must be weird being one o' them fans like Max, spending your life just following t'club around.

LEE: Dedication! Don't see enough of it these days! Too many fair-weather supporters! Too many upstarts! Look promising when they're young, then don't last five minutes. It's like Bill Shankly said that time: 'Football isn't a matter of life and death; it's more important than that.' Anyway, are we going out?

TERRY: Out where?

LEE: Plenty of clubs, aren't there, round here?

TERRY: Night clubs?

LEE: Thought we'd stroll out for a few drinks. Always used to, night before a big game. Have a dance, work some of the tension off. Your territory. You must know what's what.

TERRY: Well, there's t'Barracuda, or t'Chiarascuro . . .

LEE: (*Taking out a packet of cigarettes and removing the Cellophane*) You wanna give 'em a bell, then? See what's on? Room service'll give you the number.

TERRY: I thought we'd to stay in t'hotel?

LEE: Who says?

TERRY: Des were saying . . .

LEE: He has to say something, doesn't he? Wouldn't have a job if you took his little rule-book away from him.

TERRY: He's us boss though, int he?

LEE: Is he? Buggered if a geriatric messenger-boy's telling me how to get ready for a big match. We're class players, Terry! Professionals, not bleeding schoolkids. It's only bread-and-butter johnnies with no imagination who need rules. Cigarette?

TERRY: I don't smoke.

LEE: Try one! Used to cadge 'em off that doorman when you were a paper boy, didn't you?

TERRY: Give it up since then.

LEE: One won't harm you.

TERRY: I didn't know you smoked.

LEE: Bought 'em down in reception. No harm in one now and again. You going to get on that phone, then?

TERRY: Is it right, t'night before a game?

LEE: Course it's right if we want to do it! I was gonna have that receptionist up here at first – Wilma.

TERRY: Up here?

LEE: More fun to go out though really, wouldn't it?

TERRY: What happens if you get caught?

LEE: You don't get caught! Provided you're careful, don't do anything stupid. Jesus! I didn't expect all this! Thought you'd jump at it. Chance to go out on the tiles in your home town, get to know a few of the lads. Cos Max'd be game, and Lloyd an' Jimmy . . .

TERRY: Yeah, but . . .

LEE: Never know, might meet some of your old mates in there.

TERRY: That's a point.

LEE: No good sitting around worrying about tomorrow. Go on – have a fag!

TERRY: No, you're all right. (*Beat.*) Time would we get back?

LEE: Half two, three . . . depends who we meet. You worried about getting your beauty sleep?

TERRY: It's not that.

LEE: Prefer a quiet night in perhaps, do you? Watch television, read the paper. (*Throws* TERRY *the paper.*) Here you are!

TERRY: Tut! Don't know what's best.

LEE: You'll be all right like that – keep your tie on. Do you the world o' good. (*Beat.*) You gonna ring them or not?

TERRY: I best say no, Lee.

LEE: You corky little pillock!

TERRY: I don't want to queer my pitch. It's a big day for me tomorrow. You go.

LEE: How can I go on my own? Got to look after you, haven't I? See you get off to sleep all right without wetting the bed.

TERRY: I'll be all right.

LEE: I'd have brought my *Greyhound* magazines to catch up on if I'd known I was going to have to babysit. (*Putting cigarettes away and pouring more Perrier*) Bloody hell! Read your paper – go on!

TERRY: I'm not stopping you, Lee.

LEE: I know! I know! Don't worry, Terry! I'll sit in with you and keep you company. Bad as being at home.

(LEE *sits down, and there is a pause while things settle and* TERRY *opens the paper.*)

TERRY: Oh no!

LEE: What?

TERRY: Closing Mosborough and Totley down. Three hundred men laid off. I had a mate at Totley. Pit electrician. Used to play in a Sunday league together.

LEE: Have something to fill his free time in then, won't he? (*Beat.*) Find out what's happening in the golf.

TERRY: (*Turning the pages*) There's a match preview here. Have you read it?

LEE: I don't read that trash! Parasites on the game, reporters. (*Beat.*) What's it say?

TERRY: Oh, there's somat about me! (*Reads*:) 'Only the third appearance this season of Terry Bishop, a revelation when he came on as substitute at Coventry two weeks ago. Let us hope we see more of this promising youngster.' Fuckin' 'ell! I'm in t'*Yorkshire Post*!

LEE: All about you, is it?

TERRY: Er . . . No! You're in it, an' all.

LEE: Oh!

TERRY: (*Reads*:) 'Hillsborough will hold its breath in anti . . . antic . . .'

LEE: Anticipation.

TERRY: '. . . anticipation when Merter walks on centre stage . . .'

LEE: Load o' crap!

TERRY: 'The problem will be, as so often of late, "Will he remember his lines?"'

LEE: Eh?

TERRY: 'With younger players around him to provide the pace though, Dawes can be forgiven for turning a blind eye to his increasing waywardness. At least for the time being.'

LEE: Who's written . . .?

TERRY: 'Merter must start asking himself some serious questions if he thinks his unreliable elegance justifies a regular . . .'

LEE: (*Grabbing paper from* TERRY) Let's have a . . . (*Reads.*) Crap! Every word of it! 'Ronnie Farraday, Northern Sports Journalist of the Year'! Probably one of those wankers at school who had all the kit and couldn't kick a ball straight. We had one: Adrian Steele. Never used to have a shower cos his bollocks hadn't dropped. Has a column in one o' those football mags now. 'Men of Steele' or something.

TERRY: Oh, I read that!

LEE: Had about as much spunk in him as the Singing Nun! (*Picks phone up.*) 'Waywardness'! Means I don't run round like a rabid dog for ninety minutes like the rest of 'em. Same when I got the England drop. 'Erratic genius', it was then. (*Into phone*) Outside line! (*Dials.*)

TERRY: How many caps did you get?

LEE: Seven. Got three goals.

TERRY: Not bad.

LEE: England! They rave about the Brazilians, then put drayhorses in the team. Need a few showjumpers in there. A Paul Breitner or two. 'Lone Wolf,' they called him. Roamed around, did nothing all game, then scored a blinder just when it mattered. Born in the wrong country, me.

TERRY: There's some good players coming through now though.

LEE: There's always good players coming through! I was a good player coming through seven years ago. Any flair and they call you a name for the future and you're dropped. Got to be predictable to get on here. Fuck 'em, anyway! Dig their own grave! (*Into phone*) Hello, Eric? Oh no, it's that sodding machine! Come on! Come on! Get to the tone! Eric? It's Lee. I just rung back to ask if you'd heard anything. Give us a bell, OK? (*Slams phone down.*)

TERRY: What you keep ringing your agent for?

LEE: Never you mind!

TERRY: Is it owt to do with that Bruges thing Des were saying?

LEE: (*Contemptuously*) Des! (*Beat.*) I suppose that's why you don't want to come out, is it?

TERRY: Why?

LEE: Taste of honey when you're not used to it. Perhaps as well. No knowing what it might lead to.

TERRY: How do you mean?

LEE: I was thinking of how you used to run away.

TERRY: That were years ago.

LEE: You must have a few old flames up here, don't you?

TERRY: One or two. What . . .?

LEE: You could go to them. They'd put you up. Lie low for a few weeks till the end of the season. No one'd find you.

TERRY: What you on about?

LEE: There was a Swedish bloke once. Swimmer. Spent three years getting ready for the Tokyo Olympics. Then four days before his event he got on a plane for California. Manager had to go out looking for him. Never found him. Wife got a postcard once from Disneyland, but apart from that . . . Probably still out there, working in a bank somewhere.

TERRY: I'm not with you, Lee.

LEE: What was that club? Barracuda? Don't have to make a final decision now. Could wait till you get there. Have a drink and decide then what to do. Only a phone call away, Terry. I wouldn't tell anyone.

(TERRY *looks at the phone for a few seconds, then explodes.*)

TERRY: You want your bloody head examining, you! Think I'm gonna run off t'night before t'game that's gonna give me my break? Not that daft!

LEE: (*Going into bathroom*) Suit yourself!

TERRY: Not Lord bloody Lucan!

(TERRY *resumes the newspaper, then the phone rings.*)

(*Alarmed*) Phone's just rung, Lee!

LEE: (*Off*) Answer it, then!

TERRY: Who do you think it is?

LEE: (*Off*) Hurry up, Terry! It's an important call, that, for me. My agent.

(*It rings again and* TERRY *picks it up.*)

TERRY: Hello? Er, he's in the bathroom brushing his teeth.

LEE: (*Off*) Bloody hell!

TERRY: Shall I go call him? What? (*Listens, a little bemused.*) Yeah, all right. Can you just hold on for a minute?

(LEE *comes back on urgently, drying his hands on a towel.*)

LEE: Good old Eric! Probably had it on the machine to keep the loonies at bay.

TERRY: It were a woman.

LEE: (*Stopping dead*) Woman?

TERRY: Room service, wanting to know if everything's all right.

(LEE *retreats nervously, signalling to* TERRY *to put her off.* TERRY *is at first surprised by this, then affects to not understand, clearly enjoying* LEE*'s resulting panic.*)

(*Loud, to* LEE) Don't you want to speak to her?

LEE: (*Recoiling at the gaffe, whispering to* TERRY) Put it down!

TERRY: Is it that Wilma bird you were telling me about?

LEE: (*Recoiling still more*) Tell her I'm in the bath!

TERRY: Where? Oh aye! (*Into phone*) Hello? He's just got into the bath. Yes, all right. I'll tell him. (*Puts phone down.*) She says tell him to hurry up or his orange juice'll go flat.

LEE: Jesus Christ, Terry!

TERRY: I thought you wanted her up here?

LEE: I decide who comes in here and who doesn't! Been trying to get shot of her all evening. 'kin 'ell! Some friend, aren't you?

(LEE *starts to put his jacket on.*)

TERRY: Are y'off out?

LEE: I'm trying to relax before tomorrow and I can't even breathe in this place. They been on the phone at me all evening. They been pumping rock music at me through the floorboards stopping me from thinking. There's that TV comedian getting champagne treatment up in the penthouse suite while I'm crawling round on the floor trying to find a socket that works. Gonna be filing a complaint next week about this, don't you worry! Where's that folder? (*Gets folder and searches urgently through it.*) Can't even walk out on to the corridor without one of Dawesy's spies writing your name down in a little black book. (*Finding the right page*) Here! (*Reads*) 'Cumberland Hotel. Head Office . . .' (*Rips page out.*) That's going straight to Eric! He can throw the book at them. Sunday-paper job. (*Tries to fold it but is too furious to manage.*) Nobody treats me like this and gets away with it. Come on! Fucking paper! (*Unable to fold it he screws it up instead.*) Stuff it, anyway! Can wait till morning. I'm off!

TERRY: Where you gonna go?

LEE: I'll find somewhere, don't worry, Tel. I'll drop you a line.
(*Exit* LEE. TERRY *paces round anxiously, then tries restlessly to read the paper. Unable to concentrate, he finally picks up the phone.*)

TERRY: (*Into phone*) Er, can I speak to Des, please? Er, Wilton, Des Wilton: He's staying in the hotel. I don't know his number, he didn't . . . He's with the team. He's the trainer. Des. There's a problem, you see and . . . Thank you. (*Waits.*) No answer? Can you tell me what room number . . .? Two-four-seven. Right, thank you. Thanks. Thank you.
(TERRY *puts the phone down, thinks anxiously, then straightens his tie and exits. After a few moments* LEE *comes back on, casually drinking an orange juice. He starts to undress. Re-enter* TERRY *in a fluster.*)
Oh, you're here!

LEE: (*Sarcastic*) Yes.

TERRY: Thought you'd gone out to a club or somat.

LEE: Must be joking! Sitting in a room full of smoke, drinking gnat's piss till three in the morning? Gave them tricks up years ago. (*Beat.*) Where you been then?

TERRY: I been looking for Des.

LEE: He's down in the bar. What you want him for?

TERRY: Tell him about thee! I were worried.

LEE: I just been down to get an orange juice.

TERRY: You coulda said!

LEE: Were you worried, Terry?

TERRY: Bloody well wa!

LEE: (*Non-sarcastic*) Oh, I'm touched! (*Beat.*) I had a look at the fire-escapes on the way up. Don't look as if they've been used for years. Wouldn't fancy struggling with them locks with flames licking round me. Be a right towering inferno.
(TERRY *looks at* LEE, *bemused and still a little flustered, then goes into the bathroom while* LEE *continues to undress.*)

TERRY: (*Coming back on, indicating main light*) Do you want this off?

LEE: Might as well.
(TERRY *puts the main light off, leaving only a bedside lamp on. They undress and get into bed.*)
(*Complaining*) Single beds!

TERRY: Don't you like 'em? Been a change for me since I

moved down London, sleeping in my own bed. Used to have to sleep with our Jerry.

LEE: In the same bed?

TERRY: Our Christine as well till she were 13. Bought her one of her own then.

LEE: Should hope so! Who you in digs with, then?

TERRY: Mrs Consterdine.

LEE: Lovely lady! Looked after me once upon a time. She still a stickler for lights out?

TERRY: She's a bit funny about having people back.

LEE: I know. Likes her lads to get plenty of sleep. How do you go on, then?

TERRY: What for?

LEE: That little lottery girl I seen you with.

TERRY: Lorraine? She's not a lottery girl.

LEE: I thought I saw her wearing one o' them orange sashes one day?

TERRY: That's just her dress.

LEE: But how do you go on, then?

TERRY: What for?

LEE: Go to her mum's, do you? When they're out?

TERRY: Sometimes.

LEE: (*Chuckles.*) You're just at that age. Few first-team appearances and they'll be throwing themselves at you. Wait till you go to some of those club functions.

TERRY: I'm not interested in anyone else. We've made a pact, anyway, me and Lorraine.

LEE: Well, get it unpacked then! Look at George Best! They say he had over a thousand birds! Match days an' all! Said it gave his game an extra bit o' pep. Used to go into his boutique asking for it. (*Beat.*) Or take me and Wilma.

TERRY: You were laying eggs when she rang up!

LEE: No, but I had a very pleasant evening with her a few years back.

TERRY: Did you go through it?

LEE: She's not a turnstile, Terry! That's the trouble, though. You give 'em it once, then you're saddled. Used to be one from Harlow followed me all over. Must have spent a fortune in hotel bills. Turned up in Madrid once, night before a European semi. Hope Wilma's not gonna start that game. No harm in it once in a while, though.

TERRY: What about your wife?

LEE: What about her? You get bored with each other, you know. Couple of years and a few kids.

TERRY: It won't happen to us.

LEE: You wait! They start rationing out the sex. There's nothing left to talk about . . . God knows what I'm going to do when I hang my boots up. Least I can get away most weekends at the moment. One reason why I bought the dog.

TERRY: What kind o' dog you got?

LEE: Greyhound. Professional racer.

TERRY: Oh, I'll look out for it. What's it called?

LEE: 'Beat the Clock'. Steph wanted to call him 'Warren's Dream' after the boy but I thought it sounded a bit too poetic for a dog. But he gives us a common interest, see? Cos she won't talk about football.

TERRY: Won't she?

LEE: Only time she's been to see me is the two cup finals I been in. And they have to then, the women. Have their hair done together the same morning, sit together in a little huddle at the match. Anybody who don't go's a snob. I scored the only goal four years ago. She says at the reception, 'Who won?' I says, 'What you think that silver thing over there is? A fucking ice-bucket?'

TERRY: Lorraine's training to be hairdresser.

LEE: Yeah, well, you want someone with a bit o' class. Going to be moving in high circles in a year or two's time. Don't want some slag showing you up every time she opens her mouth.

TERRY: Is that what yours does?

LEE: She bleedin well doesn't, no! Some of the lads' wives though . . .

TERRY: What's she do?

LEE: Looks after the house. Important job when there's kids around. Good mother – I'll give her that. Beautician when I met her. Worked on health farm George took us to once. Out in Essex somewhere . . . Jesus!

TERRY: 's up?

LEE: (*Getting out of bed and limping round the room*) Bleeding foot!

TERRY: Do you really think you'll be out tomorrow?

LEE: Be having it amputated if it . . . Jesus! (*Lightly*) You'll buy me a ticket for the big matches, won't you, when I'm old and forgotten?

TERRY: Eh?

LEE: Can't go on forever.

TERRY: What about all t'money you've made?

LEE: Soon goes. Big house, foreign holidays, school fees, the dog . . .

TERRY: How did you get started, Lee?

LEE: (*Pours more Perrier*) Used to play for East London Schoolboys. Few of us went for trials. I got asked to sign up when I left school. Had a lot of trouble with my old man, though. He wanted me on the papers with him. Printers – they earn a fortune. He kept going on about the insecurity. Then he said he'd kick me out of the house if I went against his wishes. He used to hate football, the cunt!

TERRY: Didn't you like your dad?

LEE: You what!

TERRY: What about your mam?

LEE: She just did what he told her. (*Sits on bed.*) Anyway, I went and talked to George. He said leave it for a year till I was 16 – see if they melted. It was no better though, so I pissed off. Signed a contract – didn't need their consent, see, at 16 – and George put me in digs with Mrs C. Should have seen his face when I told him! He went up the wall! Told me never to come back again.

TERRY: Honest?

LEE: I was glad to get out. I didn't know if I really wanted to be a footballer, to tell you the truth. Then. He didn't want me to, though. That was a sweet enough reason. Every time I scored a goal I used to think, 'There you are, you fucker! Another smack in your face!' He came round a bit when I started making it, when he could brag about me to his mates. Never encouraged me though, when it mattered. Not like yours. I had it all to do myself. Only bloke who ever helped me was George. Him and Mrs Consterdine. Saints, both of 'em. (*Getting back into bed*) You got a lot to thank your old man for.

TERRY: I know. Be letting myself down tomorrow if I don't give hundred per cent for him. And mi old mates. They don't have much fun. Still, can't afford to hold yourself back.

LEE: Can you hear that noise? Poom! Poom! Poom!

TERRY: Can't hear owt.

LEE: Must be my ears – come out in sympathy with the dog. You don't snore, do you?

TERRY: I move about a bit.

LEE: In the room?

TERRY: In bed. Finish up wi' all t'sheets on t'floor sometimes. (*Kisses pillow loudly.*) Night anyway, love.

LEE: Eh?

TERRY: I'm kissing t'pillow and pretending it's Lorraine.

LEE: Well, make the most of it. Five years' time you'll be kissing her and wishing it was the pillow!

TERRY: Never!

LEE: You'll see. (*Beat.*) You locked the door, didn't you?

TERRY: Er . . . not sure . . .

LEE: You was the last in.

TERRY: I know, but . . . int it automatic?

LEE: Get out! Go on!

(TERRY *gets out of bed.*)

Put the light on!

(TERRY *puts it on.*)

Right. First you lock!

(TERRY *locks the door.*)

Then it's lights!

(TERRY *turns the lights off.*)

Then you get into bed.

TERRY: (*Getting into bed*) I thought you'd . . .

LEE: Yeah, well, you know what Thought did! Bloody apprentices! Training all week, nursing this foot, then I nearly go to bed with the flaming door open!

TERRY: Sorry!

LEE: You want to be inside on a night like tonight. Tight and warm. Hatches battened. Never know who might walk in!

TERRY: Do they get intruders?

LEE: There's some weird people about. See 'em sometimes through the hotel curtains, flitting about in the street light. Anyway, with your record for doing a runner . . .

TERRY: Give o'er! (*Beat.*) Eh, I'm scared now. Hits you when you're in bed, doen't it? What's gonna happen tomorrow, I mean.

LEE: You'll be all right.

TERRY: Mi big day . . . Mi place to play for, apart from owt else. Contract runs out in June. Mr Dawes says he'll talk about renewing it in a couple o' weeks. Got to prove I'm worth it first, though. Be back on t'dole otherwise. 'Graham', I mean. Not 'Mr Dawes'. Why don't you like him, Lee? Always says hello. Meant a lot to me, that, when I first came down. Missed mi mam an' dad then, man! Bloody hell! Should a seen me! It were murder! Didn't know anybody. It were all reet in t'day when you were all together up at t'ground . . . It were t'weekends. After t'match when you had all day Sunday to look forward to on your own. That's why I started running back home Saturday neets. (*Beat.*) Lee? are you asleep?

LEE: Noy yer . . .

TERRY: I'm all right now, though. Been a godsend meeting Lorraine in that respect. Tell you that much. Can't wait till we get married. No more snogging in t'back o' t'Escort then. Be able to go home together to us own furniture. (*Sighs.*) Them Question and Answer Circles are good, aren't they? I think it's right what Graham were saying about overconfidence. Just cos they're not doing that well in t'League . . . Always a good cup team, Leicester. (*Beat.*) What do you think, Lee? Do you think I'm doing all right? Do you reckon I could make it one day? Don't see why not. Do enough training. Do a five-mile run every morning, tha knows. Except Sundays. Makes a difference to your game, stamina. They say that's what won us t'World Cup in 1966, stamina . . .

LEE: (*Softly*) Terry.

TERRY: What? (*Pause.*) What?

LEE: In case, and then stand in for . . . (*Clicks his tongue a few times.*) Correction. Make that . . .

TERRY: You what?

LEE: (*Raising his voice*) Must be joking! At this time o' night?

TERRY: Are you awake, Lee?

LEE: Don't ask me, Des! Bloody hell!

TERRY: (*Amused*) Eh, Lee! You're talking in . . .

LEE: At my age? Think I am? Ask Terry! It's what he's here for! It's only half an hour from Heathrow. Not as if . . . Oh, all right then! (*Makes spitting noises.*)

TERRY: Are you all right, Lee?

LEE: No, don't go, Des! I was only joking! (*Sits up in bed and heads imaginary balls.*) You don't believe me, do you? Look! Look at that! That's why! Where are you going?

TERRY: Lee, do you . . . ?

LEE: (*Screams*) I didn't mean it! (*Wakes up, blinking.*)

TERRY: Are you OK, Lee?

LEE: Was I shouting?

TERRY: Something about Heathrow . . .

LEE: (*Dismissive*) Yeah, I do that sometimes. Specially before a big game. I didn't wake you up, did I?

TERRY: No.

LEE: Must have been the roly-poly. (*Settles down in bed.*) Night anyway, Tel. We locked the door, didn't we?

TERRY: Yeah. Yeah, it's locked.

LEE: In for the night now, then. Sleep well.

TERRY: (*Still disturbed*) Yeah. (*Pause, then finally settles down in bed.*) And you.

(*Darkness.*)

ACT TWO

SCENE ONE

Park. A sunny morning the next day.
DES, *in tracksuit, with stopwatch, is setting out a row of footballs. He keeps looking at someone offstage.*

DES: Come on! Put some weight on it! Only way to try it out.
(*Enter* LEE *in tracksuit, running.*)
Not bad. How did it feel at full stretch?
LEE: So-so.
DES: Stand on your bad foot, then. Lift the other. Higher! Turn it around like a clock. And down. And up. Knee up to your chin – go on! And down. Now do it with the other. That's it. Now back on your right foot. Crouch down on it. Hurt?
LEE: Difficult to say.
DES: Raise yourself up. Slowly. Now do some running on the spot. Bit faster – come on! And now jumping. Fine. Now tread water. Right, I want one set o' doggies and one set o' dummies. Are you ready? Wait till I give the instruct– Go!
(LEE *does the doggies and returns.*)
Not bad. One, two, three, four, five, six, seven, eight, nine, don't antici– Go!
(LEE *does the dummies and returns.*)
Good. See what you're like on the ball then.
(DES *picks the first ball up and throws it to* LEE.)
Control it! Shoot!
(LEE *controls it and shoots.* DES *picks the second ball up and throws it.*)
Volley!
(LEE *volleys the ball away.* DES *points to the third ball.*)
Lee Merter special! Go on! Punish it!
(LEE *thunders the last ball off.*)
Good.
(DES *picks up a loose ball.*)
All right?
(DES *puts the ball between himself and* LEE *so they are both about two yards away from it. Brief pause.*)
Whose is it?
(*They both go for the ball and meet in a crunching tackle, but*

LEE *wins through*.)

Not bad! How does it feel?

LEE: Well, it's not actually hurting, but . . .

DES: But what?

LEE: Dunno.

DES: How did it feel in the tackle?

LEE: Didn't feel too bad.

DES: Stand on it again.

(LEE *does so, and* DES *gets down to examine it*.)

What was it like kicking the ball?

LEE: Felt more or less normal.

DES: How's that?

LEE: All right.

DES: Feel anything now?

LEE: No . . .

DES: Anything there?

(LEE *shakes his head*.)

Or there?

LEE: It's more like pain's going to start than actually feeling anything now.

DES: (*Getting up*) Does it hurt, Lee? Or not?

LEE: Well . . .

DES: Yes or no?

LEE: Not really.

DES: Cos I can't find anything wrong with you. How you feeling in yourself?

LEE: Not bad. Had a bit of a rough night.

DES: Music keep you awake?

LEE: Mmm . . . hard to say.

DES: Do you feel tired?

LEE: Don't exactly feel tired . . .

DES: Do you want to play? Let's put it that way.

LEE: What do you think?

DES: It's you I'm asking! Bloody hell! Like asking the wife what she wants for Christmas.

LEE: Could chance it, I suppose.

DES: Cos as far as I'm concerned you're a hundred per cent.

LEE: It was twingeing.

DES: Is it twingeing now?

LEE: Don't seem to be.

DES: So what's your problem?

LEE: I don't want to play and get taken off. Don't want to let anyone down.

DES: I've given you a comprehensive workout. If you had any reason not to play you'd sure as sports mixtures be feeling it now.

LEE: Yeah?

DES: You wouldn't have been able to twist and turn for a start, let alone kick a ball. And that tackle would have put you out for a couple o' weeks. I wouldn't say if I thought you wasn't up to it, Lee. Can't afford to take risks like that in a semi. Your decision though. Can't force you to play.

LEE: What if it comes back in the game?

DES: What if the main stand collapses? What if they drop the bomb on Sheffield in injury time? Cross that bridge when we come to it. No reason why it should, anyway. And we'll need you out there today – tell you that much. Presence you've got. Put the fear of God into 'em.

LEE: Yeah?

DES: They'd be cock-a-hoop if they knew you wasn't playing. Give 'em all the confidence in the world. Play O'Neill as sweeper – he'd have a field day. And there's our youngsters to think about. Blokes like Terry with no experience at this level. Gonna be shitting bricks in the first ten minutes. Be looking to you to hold 'em together.

LEE: I'm not that important!

DES: Don't you underestimate yourself. Your name on a team sheet still got a lot of clout. 'Erratic genius' – remember when they was calling you that?

LEE: That was years ago.

DES: Once a genius . . . I'd say forty per cent of their energy'll be going on to worrying about you if you play. That's nearly half.

LEE: You reckon?

DES: I'm sure.

LEE: Just test it again.

DES: (*Getting down to the foot*) How's that?

LEE: Don't feel too bad actually.

DES: I'm gonna apply pressure on that tendon. Ready?

LEE: Yeah – go on.

DES: (*Working the foot round*) Feel anything?

LEE: Nah.

DES: Now?
LEE: I mean I can feel pressure from your hand.
DES: I hope so! Be taking you down the mortuary if you couldn't feel that! There's no pain?
LEE: Not a thing.
DES: (*Getting up*) Clean as a whistle.
LEE: No, I don't feel too bad at all.
DES: What's it going to be, then?
LEE: I reckon I'll be all right.
DES: I'll put you down then?
LEE: Yeah. Put me down.
DES: Good man!
LEE: Nothing the matter with me.

(LEE *paces around, more confidently now, doing a few more exercises.*)

DES: So let's see . . . Leaves us at full strength apart from Noel. Terry goes in for him, and Wayne can go number 12.
LEE: In fact it feels stronger than the left foot after those exercises.
DES: Supposed to be your strongest. Favour it, don't you?
LEE: How about them? They got any problems?
DES: Not as far as we know. Graham brought some programmes back from the ground. Had a look at the pitch. Dried out a bit since last night, thank God! Just hope it stays like this.
LEE: Beautiful morning.
DES: Oh, you've noticed now, have you?
LEE: (*Playing with the ball*) 'And it's Merter, Merter so dangerous from these set pieces. Can he curl this . . . ? Oh, it's there! He done it! Beautiful ball! One–nil!'
DES: That's more like it!
LEE: Play better in adversity – always said so. Remember my first semi-final. Nil–nil at half-time. Been having a terrible game – walking round in a dream most of the time. Just couldn't get into it. We were going off for the break and one of their lottery girls was standing by the tunnel. Hot pants, skimpy little T-shirt, giving me this 'come-on' look. So I smiles back. I thought, you know, maybe I haven't had such a bad game after all. Then, just as I'm walking past her, she leans forward, still smiling, and says, 'Fuck off, you cockney wanker!' Just like that! Whispers it like, so's no one else could hear. She really got to me, though. I

went into the changing room like my bollocks had been snipped off. Made her pay for it in the second half though. Thundered in a twenty-five-yard volley, saw us to Wembley. Talk about a shot fired in anger! Went through their defence like a nail bomb!

DES: That's what we need! Eh, Lee! Listen! Can you hear it? (*Chanting off of fans singing 'There's only one Lee Merter' to the tune of 'Guantanamera'.*)

LEE: They're down there! By the lake! (*Salutes them.*) Troops have started arriving already. We got the best fans in England, I reckon. Look at 'em! Must have come up last night. Good on you, men! Be there! Be there! We got fans on the terraces, fans in the park. I tell you, Des, we're gonna take this city apart today! How many you reckon'll be there?

DES: Forty thousand, forty-five. I can remember when you'd get sixty here for a semi.

LEE: Yeah?

DES: Big footballing town like Sheffield. Lucky if they get twenty between 'em now, Wednesday and United. Same all over – empty terraces.

LEE: They should get their finger out if they got problems. We had to when we went down to the second that time.

DES: We had money, though. Even worse now. Got to be rich these days or you've had it. Only about seven clubs solvent in the country.

LEE: They can't expect others to keep baling 'em out. (LEE *makes as if to kick the ball off to the fans but* DES *snatches it from him.*)

DES: Eh! Twenty quid a time, then! Dock it from your wages!

LEE: That's what it's about though, isn't it? The big gesture. They'll tell their grandchildren about that.

DES: It's what it used to be about. Belt-tightening time now, Lee. George's days are over.

LEE: We'll have to do some resurrecting then this afternoon. Won't we?
(*They look at each other. Lights fade.*)

SCENE TWO

Changing room. That afternoon.
Sounds off of pre-match noises from stadium: fans singing; pop music and messages being relayed on the PA system; team changes being announced and fans responding accordingly.
LEE *and* TERRY *are changing into their kit.*

TERRY: Will Graham be back in?

LEE: Will he, fuck! Not till half-time. Be up in the directors' box from now on. Doesn't want to get wintergreen on his Lord John blazer, does he? No. He leaves the last bit to Des.
(*The crowd roars.*)

TERRY: Listen at that! Them ours, do you think?

LEE: Not loud enough for ours. You wait for that roar when we run out. Twenty thousand of our boys be out there today. Want blood. Our job to give 'em it an' all. Piss on them wankers! (*Sings:*) 'Don't sleep in the subway, darling!'

TERRY: Can hardly fasten mi fucking laces!

LEE: Don't worry! They'll be the same. Smell that?

TERRY: What?

LEE: Shit. Wafting over from their changing rooms. They'll need mucking out before three o'clock.

TERRY: Wish I hadn't had that egg flan though.

LEE: Quiche.

TERRY: Tha what?

LEE: 'Egg flan'! Quiche Lorraine!

TERRY: Is that what it's called?

LEE: Pass me that liniment, will you?

TERRY: I'll have to tell t'bird that. She's called Lorraine.

LEE: (*Sings:*) 'Don't stand in the pouring rain!' (*Beat.*) Do you reckon these studs'll be OK?

TERRY: Dunno. Should be.

LEE: You used to do my kit.

TERRY: I'm not a ballboy now!

LEE: Still a bit soft out there. Might need extra grip . . .
(*Enter* NOEL *with match programmes.*)

NOEL: Here you are, lads! Programmes.

LEE: What you collecting for? St John's Ambulance?

NOEL: Atmosphere out there! Incredible! Must be forty-five thousand!

LEE: Is that a police estimate, Inspector?

TERRY: (*Looking at programme*) There's my name on t'back page! Number 11: Terry Bishop.

LEE: Might be to let everyone know who you are, Terry.

NOEL: There'll be a photo of you inside.

TERRY: (*Looking*) Will there? No, it's got you in. I've never been in a first team photo . . . Oh, they've put me in a little box!

LEE: Terry's Chocolates!

TERRY: (*Reads*:) 'Inset photo: Terry Bishop'.

LEE: (*Looking*) You trying to grow a moustache when they took this?

TERRY: No.

LEE: Look like something that lives in a cave. Have you seen it, Noel? Look at them eyes! Wonder they didn't burn the camera lens out!

NOEL: You do look frightening actually, Tel. Banks'll be having fits when he sees that.

TERRY: Wild man of the peaks!

NOEL: Has Des been in?

LEE: Not yet.

NOEL: That's when you'll know it's nearly time, Terry, cos Des comes in.

TERRY: Oh, aye?

NOEL: Gives you some last-minute instructions.

LEE: He knows what he's got to do.

TERRY: Provide you an' Lloyd.

LEE: That's it.

TERRY: Get it up front.

LEE: Ooh! Why do I always think of Wilma when I hear that? I could just give her one here and now. Up against these pegs! She had a snatch like an open goal!

TERRY: Eh! Were that t'bell?

LEE: The bell! Ten minutes yet. Time to get the shits and get over 'em yet. (*Sings*:) 'But I wanna know for sure!' Eh, Lloyd! Get that tucked in! Not allowed to take blunt instruments on to the field you know! Not a shagging competition!

NOEL: All right, Lloyd?

TERRY: Feel better when I'm out there an' kicked t'ball a few times.

(LEE *gets a photograph out of his wallet and kisses it.*) Who's that?

LEE: 'Beat the Clock'.

NOEL: He always kisses it before a game.

TERRY: Let's have a look. (*Takes it.*) Who's that at t'back?

LEE: Steph.

TERRY: Nice-looking.

LEE: Yeah, he'd just had his coat trimmed.

TERRY: Steph, I mean!

LEE: Aw!

TERRY: Where were it taken?

LEE: Haringey. Last year. Won a race later that evening. Not bad going considering he had the worms.

TERRY: (*Handing it back*) Passed 'em on to me, t'state o' my guts.

NOEL: It's normal to feel nervous before a big match, Tel. And they say a bit of adrenalin lifts your game, so don't worry! One o' my first appearances was against Leicester as it happens. 's see, what year would it have been? Must have been seventy-one . . . It was! I remember cos we went on the piss after and I was still having to lie about my age. How old are you? Nineteen?

TERRY: Just, aye.

NOEL: Well, I was 17. So think what it was like for me! If you're 19 and frightened . . .

LEE: Was that when you were in the sea cadets, Noel?

NOEL: (*Ignoring* LEE) No, it was seventy-one, and it was at that time – I don't know if you remember – there was a toilet-roll shortage. Bit before your time probably . . .

LEE: (*Sings:*) 'I won't let you down . . .'

NOEL: Anyway, we'd been allowed twelve pieces each that day, but I was so nervous I'd already used up my ration and I wanted to go again. So I asked this bloke who used to play for us, Johnny Shaw – you won't remember him – if I could lend some of his. I says, 'Can you lend me some bog roll, Johnny? I've run out. I'll pay you back Monday.' And he just looked at me – I'll never forget it – (*laughing at his own joke*) he looked at me and he said, 'You're not the only one who's nervous, son! What you think I've brought yesterday's paper up with me for? To check the crossword off?'

(*Embarrassed pause.*)

See, he'd brought his *Express* up with him . . .

LEE: We know! We know! Johnny Shaw! Wonder what he's doing now? Stuffing papers down his shirt and sleeping out on the Embankment like Eddie, I suppose. Eh, Noel?

TERRY: (*Remembering*) Oh, my dad said to watch out for t'referee!

LEE: Well, there will be one, Terry, you know – football match . . .

TERRY: No, I mean, what's he like? His reputation and that.

NOEL: (*Looking at programme*) Mr Norman C. Sleaford. Can't say as I . . .

LEE: Norman C. Sleaford! Is that him. . . ? (*Gets his programme.*) It is!

TERRY: What?

LEE: From Bristol. He gave me a penalty once when I took a dive.

TERRY: What's wrong with that?

LEE: He's terrible. Sent Ian off in the same match for complaining when he'd nearly had his leg broken in half. I'm telling you, he's a disaster area!

TERRY: Oh, no!

LEE: And he hates London.

TERRY: That's all we needed.

LEE: Few stories I've heard about him being bent. Haven't you, Noel?

NOEL: Norman C. Sleaford . . .

TERRY: He looked all right to me.

LEE: When did you see him?

TERRY: Talking to Graham.

LEE: Big fat bloke with red hair and a beard?

TERRY: No, he were little and going bald.

LEE: I'm thinking of a different feller.

TERRY: You bloody get!

(*Enter* DES *in tracksuit and carrying an aeroplane propeller.*)

DES: All right! All right! Settle down! Save that for out there!

LEE: Wheyhey, Des! Shooting off early, are you?

NOEL: Was it raining up there, Des?

LEE: Is that so you can get up to Dawesy and tell him what's happening?

DES: I thought I might fix it to the ceiling actually – cool things down a bit in here. (*Puts it on the bench.*) Local flying club. Want you comedians to sign it. Hospital charity or something.

NOEL: You didn't tear the pitch up landing, did you?

DES: I'll sign your plaster later, Noel. Just sit in the corner somewhere and suck a boiled sweet while I talk to these lads. OK?

(NOEL *reluctantly slips to the sidelines while* DES *moves to address the team as a whole.*)

So, you got eight minutes. All heard what Graham said. We want this one perfect. Want the right attitude from the word go. Spirit of Bayern Munich eighty-two. Go out and play like you're two goals down already. Close 'em down in the middle and tear their back four wide open. All right, Terry?

TERRY: Yeah.

DES: (*Massaging* TERRY'*s legs*) Don't let Banks settle on the ball. And watch out for that number 4. He's only a little shirt-pulling wanker so don't be scared of him. Go in hard! He'll soon cry off. But Banks is the man. Don't let him settle or it could be curtains. Nervous?

TERRY: Bit, yeah.

DES: So will they be, don't worry! Few pairs of brown shorts among their lot or I'm a fucking Arsenal supporter. You're gonna have a great game today, OK?

TERRY: Are they gonna be playing wide down t'flanks, do you think?

DES: You just close 'em down in the middle and provide your front men! Never mind what their plans are! We're calling the tune today, not them. And watch for the odd chance to run in from deep if you think there's something on. Look for the space. They won't be expecting it so much from you, you see? Have a crack and show Lee how it should be done. He thinks he's a smart player. All right? (*Gets up.*) Where's your partner in crime? (*Goes across to another part of the room.*) Ian!

DES: (*Continuing under dialogue*) All right for Borodin? Don't leave him in space. That's the secret

NOEL: (*To* TERRY) It's good, isn't it, when he does your legs?

TERRY: Not bad, aye.

with him. He's from Poland, remember, so he'll soon get used to having his fucking freedom restricted. I want martial rule imposed by half-time, OK? Bury your man before he gets going.

NOEL: Relaxes you, I always think. Mind you, I think a lot of it's psychological, you know. All in the mind. Don't you, Lee?

LEE: Have you seen my tie-ups anywhere, Terry?

TERRY: Aren't they under your towel?

DES: Goes for all of you! I want corpses! Haven't come up here to watch football – I've come to see a fucking funeral. How's that foot, Lee?

LEE: Fine.

DES: (*Massaging* LEE*'s legs*) You'll be all right. Just remember, they'll be terrified of you. Probably put O'Neill on you.

LEE: 's what I thought, yeah – O'Neill.

DES: He's dogged. Just pull him out wide and get behind him. You'll lose him easy on the turn, no sweat. And he's pushing 30 remember!

LEE: Not like me, eh?

DES: Put it this way. He'll need that Lucozade he's been advertising by the time you've finished with him. And don't be afraid of striking it! Have a go! Better to have struck and missed than never to have . . . know what I mean? Young Terry's looking goal-hungry this afternoon. Don't want an apprentice like him showing you up, do you? Let's have a few of them nail bombs you were talking about this morning. (*Getting up and addressing them all*) I want commitment! Don't want any shirkers! All right, captain?

DES: (*Going off to talk to another individual and continuing under dialogue*) Leadership, son, OK? Juggle things around a bit if you think they're not working, but don't go crazy! (*To all*) Pure and simple, this one. I want to be able to phone Arthur on Monday

NOEL: (*To* TERRY) What's the first thing you gonna do when you get out there?

TERRY: I don't know!

NOEL: First thing I normally do is strike a few shots at Chris. Give him a feel of the ball. Then I look to see which of their lot's got his eyes on me. That tells you who's gonna be

morning and book the coach for the twenty-first of May: Hertford to Wembley Park, one way. So good solid football. As long as you keep your names out of the book. Hear that, Jimmy? On eighteen points, don't forget, you. Just walk away from it if there's trouble, crucifix or not round your neck. Kiss it any more and you'll get lead poisoning. No, you'll be all right. How's your vocals, Lloyd? Want to hear you screaming for that ball. Don't worry if they start throwing PG Tips on the pitch – it's their problem if they got fans who can't tell a chimp from a gorilla. Scream for it! OK?

marking you. Course you don't have to do that. Probably got your own system, have you? Just helps me a bit. Are you excited?

TERRY: Bit.

LEE: Shouldn't you be out there, Noel, controlling the crowd?

NOEL: Eh?

LEE: Be useful, wouldn't it? Get a bit of first-hand experience if you're gonna be a copper.

NOEL: Go bollocks, Lee!

LEE: I'm sure Graham'd let you off for the afternoon. Day release.

NOEL: I just want to wish Tel all the best.

LEE: I know! Show him there's no hard feelings.

DES: (*Coming over from Lloyd*) You hear that, Terry?

TERRY: What?

DES: You washed your ears out this morning?

TERRY: I were listening to Noel.

DES: I'm saying to Lloyd to scream for the ball. You're the provider. I don't want him and Lee coming in at half-time complaining about ball deprivation. I want 'em bloated. OK?

TERRY: Yeah, right.

DES: Important job, that. Now where's Dean?

DES: (*Walking off again to another part of the room and continuing under dialogue*) All right for Lineker, Dean? Just steer him into the corners if he

NOEL: (*To* TERRY) He usually says that to me, that line about . . .

TERRY: Oh, fuck off, Noel, will you! I'm trying to get fucking ready!

starts running into dangerous . . .

LEE: Yeah, Noel! You've made your point. There's no hard feelings even though he's wearing your shirt. You're a big-hearted feller. Now, fuck off, will you!

DES: Hey! Hey! What's going off?

LEE: (*To* NOEL) Trying to get psyched up here!

NOEL: (*To* DES) I just said to Terry that you usually . . .

DES: (*To* NOEL) Out!

NOEL: I only wanted to . . .

DES: Out! Go on! Should never have been in here!

(*Exit* NOEL.)

(*To* TERRY) All right, prince?

TERRY: Yeah, I'm sorry. I just blew . . .

DES: It's all right, it's all right. Just keep it bubbling under. Let it spill out out there. You'll give 'em the shock of their lives.

LEE: Been getting on my tits all weekend with that arm. Dunno what Dawesy's playing about at bringing him up here for a semi.

DES: All right, he's gone now.

LEE: Putting us all off balance. Must want us to lose.

DES: Just remember, Terry, what I was saying about providing your front men. Plenty of good ball. Give it and go! Give it and go! And give 'em the option. Gonna score, anyway, aren't we, Lee?

LEE: We are if we can get into a decent frame of mind.

DES: I can see it, actually. I think you could get a couple this afternoon. Like I say, have a go! Don't be scared. Take your time on the set pieces. They start panicking, this lot, if it looks like you've something up your sleeve. Now where's John the Baptist? (*Looks round.*) You understand what I'm saying? Comprensez? Avanti! All right? I want some fucking avanti this afternoon from you!

LEE: He's not a Dago, Des. He's a Frog.

DES: He understands. Nodding his head, anyway. That's it! Goals! Bootees! (*To all*) And think about me while you're out there. I have the wife to contend with all day Sunday if we lose, complaining she lives in a morgue. (*To* LEE) What you keep looking at your studs for?

LEE: Just checking 'em.

DES: Are you sure you don't want to slip out and inspect the pitch again just to make sure? We can delay the start for ten minutes.

LEE: I always check 'em before . . .

DES: Leave the fuckers alone, will you! I want some magic from you today. Should be able to go out there in wellingtons and slot 'em in. (*To all*) I want plenty of scrap today. English semi-final, this, remember! Not a South American exhibition match. So cut out the fancy work! I want danger. Not that fucking virtuoso stuff!

DES: (*Continuing under Lee's next speech*)Tight across the back, you four! Don't rely on that offside trap too much. Could do it once too often. Watch for 'em on the break, John!

LEE: In other words, flog all over the pitch till our balls drop off. Work up a good honest sweat. Danger! Don't know the meaning of the word!

(*A bell rings, and* LEE *and* TERRY *get up.* LEE *starts to pound a ball manically against the wall, working himself up.*)

DES: All right! That's it! Up to you now. Good collective spirit! Plenty of attack! Into 'em like tigers! Good bruising tackles! Keep it clean though. And all thoughts on winning. It's what we pay you for. Good luck, Tel! Show 'em what you're made of! Look after him, Lee. Good luck, all of you! You'll do it! Kill 'em today – I can feel it. Plenty of good old-fashioned graft.

(LEE *kicks the ball to* TERRY *and checks his hair in the mirror.*)

Next game you line up for'll be at Wembley. Southside dressing room, be it Stoke or Everton.

(*The bell rings again.*)

Come on, then! Best performances, everybody! Hundred and ten per cent! Think positive and you'll piss on 'em! Into the tunnel, then! Come on! Out you get! And keep it bloody simple!

(*Exit* DES.)

LEE: They've all gone, Tel.

TERRY: I know. We better . . .

LEE: (*Taking* TERRY *by the shoulder*) It's your last chance.

TERRY: Last chance – what for?

LEE: Go look one o' those old flames up. You know all the streets round here. All the short cuts.

TERRY: Stop fucking me about, Lee! I want to . . .

LEE: I'll come with you if you like.

(*Brief pause.*)

TERRY: (*Shaking* LEE'*s hand off*) You want fucking, you!

LEE: Come on, then!

(*Exit* LEE *and* TERRY, *to roars from the crowd.*)

SCENE THREE

The same. Later that afternoon.
Sounds off of crowd responding to the game in progress. Then, indignant roars from the crowd; referee's whistle; booing; crowd goes quiet; applause; resumption of normal crowd noise.
Presently, the sound of two pairs of boots coming down the tunnel, then DES *leads on* TERRY *who has a cut eye and is in an emotional state.*

TERRY: I were all right!
DES: Come on! Lie down!
TERRY: I don't want to lie down. There's nowt up wi' me! It's only a cut! Bit o' blood wain't harm me . . .
DES: Stop messing about, Terry!
(TERRY *reluctantly allows* DES *to lie him down on the couch, but he fights it all the way.*)
TERRY: I dint want to come off! It were only for a minute I couldn't see!
DES: Look, will you just shut the rabbit and calm down! Let's have a look! (*Examines eye, applies medication, etc.*) Nasty! Bloody animal! Didn't even give him a fucking yellow card!
TERRY: It were an accident. We ran into each other.
DES: Oh, yeah? Not off the pitch though, is he? He knew what he was doing.
TERRY: He were hurt as well.
DES: Yes. I suppose he broke his elbow putting it in your eye, did he? Poor bloke. Feel sorry for him. Just keep your head still a minute!
TERRY: I went blind for a few seconds, then it were all blurred, then it were all right.
DES: Don't think it needs stitches. Roll it round a bit.
TERRY: He shouldn't have taken me off.
DES: And blink! Does it hurt?
TERRY: No, not really.
DES: Looks safe enough. I'll just put some . . .
TERRY: What did he take me off for, Des? I scored, didn't I?
DES: Just lie still, will you! Unless you want an eyeful of this! You would be jumping about then! Just . . .

(TERRY *winces in pain as* DES *applies some ointment to the eye.*)

All right, it's all right. You had a good seventy minutes. Takes it out of you at this level. League game maybe and we'd have kept you on.

TERRY: Look at me, though, Des! I'm burning up! I could do a four-minute mile and still play! I wanna go back on. I wanna score another!

DES: How can you go back on when you've been subbed? Only place you'll be going is hospital unless you quieten down a bit and give it chance to close up! Anyway, he's a good lad is Wayne. Bit of experience'll do him good. He'll be all right.

TERRY: Is that why he took me off?

DES: Why?

TERRY: To give Wayne a chance? (*Beat.*) It is, int it? Oh, fucking hell!

DES: Keep still! And calm down!

TERRY: I were playing as well as any fucker, I know I wa. There were others weren't playing as well, don't care how experienced they are. Should have taken them off. And Lee were even fucking limping. Best game I ever fucking had and you killed it!

DES: Look! For all we knew you could have cracked your skull over by that corner. You said yourself you couldn't fucking see properly. And you could hardly stand, never mind run and kick a fucking ball!

TERRY: Only for five minutes.

DES: Five minutes! It's a fucking semi-final, Terry! Can't afford to play ten men while you sit on the touchline making up your mind whether you're fit to go back on or not! It does not earn you a place on the field for ninety minutes just because you score a goal. It's a long time, that last twenty minutes, specially when you're not feeling too bright. First rule in this game is 'Make sure!' And if that means bringing off a match winner . . . Look how many times Greenwood did it with Brooking!

TERRY: He were old.

DES: Right! And you're young! Still an unknown quantity. Wouldn't even have been playing if Noel hadn't been injured, don't forget! You'll get plenty more chances.

(*Beat.*) How does that head feel?

TERRY: Eye's smarting now you've put that stuff on it.

DES: It will be. How do you feel apart from that?

TERRY: All right.

DES: Cos if you're feeling groggy or sick we best take you to the hospital and get it looked at properly.

TERRY: I don't feel sick.

DES: You sure?

TERRY: Yeah.

DES: Get your tracksuit on then and we'll go sit on the bench. Unless you'd rather lie down here?

TERRY: No, no, I'll come.

(TERRY *gets off the couch and slowly puts his tracksuit on.*)

DES: No, you'll have a bit of a shiner there. Have to ask Max for some steaks to put on it.

TERRY: I wonder what they all thought?

DES: Who?

TERRY: Mi dad, mi mates an' that. First thing that came into my head when I scored, that. And when I got taken off.

DES: Proud of you, I expect. Can you manage?

TERRY: I dint know what were happening, rect. I mean, I remember t'build-up, and scoring. Then it were all noise, like everybody jumped on me. Thought I were going deaf and suffocating all at t'same time. Next thing I knew I were back on t'half-way, taking up my position. Can't remember in between. Except that I'd scored on my home ground.

DES: Come on. Get yourself zipped up.

TERRY: Best thing I ever did in my life were that.

DES: Better than getting your end away, isn't it?

TERRY: It were fucking choz.

DES: You ready then?

TERRY: Yeah.

DES: Come on. Let's get back out. Cheer 'em on a bit. Steady now!

TERRY: I'm all right.

(*Exit* DES *and* TERRY. *The crowd roars.*)

SCENE FOUR

Coach, later that afternoon.
Two pairs of seats separated by an aisle. The coach is stationary. Sounds off of fans milling about outside. NOEL *is collecting a snack and a drink.*

NOEL: (*To fan outside*) How can I sign anything with this? Silly sods!
(NOEL *sits down. Enter presently* TERRY *in suit and tie. He collects a snack.*)
Get through all right?
TERRY: Just about.
NOEL: Bloody kids! Natural though, I suppose. I was the same. Must have been your stomping ground, was it, once upon a time?
TERRY: Used to be, aye.
NOEL: Was that your dad in the tea room?
TERRY: (*Sitting down across the aisle from* NOEL) Yeah.
NOEL: Bet he was proud of you, wasn't he? Cos that goal was a blinder. Be keeping me out of the team, if you go on. You heard Stoke beat Everton?
TERRY: (*Uninterested*) Did they?
NOEL: Two–one. Watch it on the box tonight. See what we'll be up against in the final.
TERRY: When we get there.
NOEL: We'll get there. They were lucky to get that equalizer. Bloody lucky. Can't understand what Lee was doing back in the box. How's his leg?
TERRY: Didn't seem too good.
NOEL: Hope he's all right for the replay. What about your eye?
TERRY: It's reet.
NOEL: Looks swollen. Got this plaster coming off in ten days myself, anyway, thank God!
(*More noise off from fans.*)
(*Looking out*) Here he is! Cor! It does look bad.
FAN: (*Off*) You done nothing today, Lee. Nothing! Some people work for their money, if you don't.
NOEL: Oh, God! It's him!

TERRY: Who?

NOEL: Critic in residence.

FAN: (*Off*) Do you know what it cost me to come up here? Eight pounds fifty! Plus two-fifty to get in. Plus my tube fares. Thirteen quid to watch you. And you've done nothing! Thousand quid a week you're getting. I want you to justify it!

TERRY: He's quite old, int he?

NOEL: He's only about 30.

TERRY: To be carrying on like that, I mean.

FAN: (*Off*) Come on, Lee! Cat got your tongue? I want to know why I should pay thirteen quid to get up here to watch you stroll around. And you're getting all that money.

NOEL: There's another writes letters telling us what he thinks – how we can improve our game and so on. You'll be getting one next week. 'Nice goal but could be a bit quicker dropping back' – something like that. Pain in the arse though sometimes, this one.

FAN: (*Off*) I could have worked overtime today instead of spending all that money. It's a lot to some people, thirteen quid. Might not be much to you but it's a bloody fortune to me these days.

NOEL: Aw, shut it!

TERRY: Doen't nobody ever have a go at him?

NOEL: You can't, you see. You've just to swallow your pride and accept it. Hope anyone listening'll have the sense to realize he's a bit soft in the head.

FAN: (*Off*) You were fucking rubbish! And it cost me all that money. What have you got to say for yourself? I want one good reason why I should come again to watch you. Oh, it's on to the bus, is it? There's still some autographs to sign yet, Lee! You were telling Jim Rosenthal it was every player's duty to sign autographs. Aren't you gonna sign these young lads' autographs? And you still haven't answered my question. I've a good mind to send you a bill for that thirteen quid I paid to come all the way up here to watch you . . .

(*Enter* LEE *in suit and tie, limping.*)

LEE: Windy bugger!

NOEL: Take no notice! He's cracked.

LEE: (*Getting his snack*) Ought to be banned from big games!

NOEL: There's one at every club. Don't you remember that Aston Villa supporter that time?

LEE: 'Thirteen quid it cost me to come up here!' Too tolerant for our own good sometimes. Graham should issue 'em all with ID cards. Root out undesirables like him. They do it in Russia.

NOEL: You were a model of restraint, Lee.

LEE: (*Sitting down next to* NOEL) No newspapermen around, thank God. All in the tea room. And my bloody foot's playing me up again.

NOEL: I thought I saw you limping.

LEE: Seeing the specialist on Monday. I'm sick to death of it. Be starting up my own clinic soon. (*Opening his snack and noticing* TERRY) Oh, I'm sitting next to the glory boy, I see! Flushed with success, are we? Got a right shiner there! Hope your little lottery girl can stand the sight of blood. Dirty sodding defender! I'd have had a go at him myself if it hadn't a been for this foot. How did your first interview go? Barry Davies, wasn't it?

TERRY: Yeah.

LEE: He understood you all right, then? (*To* NOEL) Be sixpence to talk to him soon.

NOEL: Great cup début, though.

LEE: Oh, yeah. Beautiful goal. Can't take that away from him. Must have lost a few pounds, did you, all that running around you did? (*Beat.*) This coach home when we haven't won! Just look at it! More action under a nun's nightie! Here! Why do you always see nuns in pairs? Each nun has to see the other nun gets none. No, I didn't think it was funny either. (*To* TERRY) Your old man told me it in the tea room. Character, isn't he? Suppose he was a bit nervous, being behind the scenes for the first time, meeting all his old heroes, sharing in his son's hour of glory . . .

TERRY: Leave him out of it.

LEE: What?

TERRY: I said, leave him out of it!

LEE: Oh, sorry!

TERRY: Owt to say about me tha can say it to mi face, but don't go picking on somebody who can't answer back for hissen.

LEE: I beg your pardon, Terry. Didn't realize I was touching on a sensitive area. I was merely commenting on the brilliance of your goal, likes o' which don't seem to have been witnessed within living memory by all accounts.

TERRY: Aye, I know. Yourn wan't bad either.

LEE: Do what?

TERRY: That little back heel you gave to Lineker. Good as a goal.

LEE: Somebody has to provide the skill.

TERRY: Can't all be showjumpers, can we?

LEE: You trying to say something, Terry?

NOEL: Cool it, Lee!

TERRY: He took me off in case I did somat daft.

LEE: You was injured.

TERRY: So were you.

LEE: Not as bad as you, I wasn't! You were out cold for ten minutes.

TERRY: Half a minute! Anyway, you might as well a been out cold, t'way you laiked. I see now why they call you a danger man!

LEE: You know, I do believe he's having a go at me, Noel. Come on then, old son! Put your dukes up! If that's what you want!

NOEL: Give it a rest, lads! Bad enough as it is without arguing.

LEE: There's me thinking you were a nice quiet lad from up north.

TERRY: Surprised you laiked at all, t'way tha were moaning an' groanin' abaht thi leg all last neet. Anybody'd a thought tha'd got trench foot, t'way tha were carrying on!

LEE: Would you mind saying that in English? I didn't quite catch it.

TERRY: Aye, go on! Take piss out o' mi accent an' where I come from!

LEE: I am doing.

TERRY: Clever wi' words, aren't you, you fucking cockneys? All wankers when it comes to t'crunch, though. Nowt but piss an' wind. Should try taking piss out o' t'goal I got.

LEE: Oh, you scored a goal, did you? Well well well! Don't often hear o' that in football. Should write a letter to the papers an' let 'em know.

TERRY: Don't hear o' thee scoring too many these days. Not for t'side you're supposed to be laikin' for anyroad.

LEE: We don't go shooting our mouths off every time we score a goal, you know! Not after we've left primary school, anyway.

TERRY: Could do wi' a bucket o'er thi head half o' t' time – stop it swelling. And God knows why! Couldn't even pot that sitter five minutes from t'end!

NOEL: Look, pack it in . . .

LEE: What do you want me to do? Lie down in front of the coach? Don't exactly feel top of the world myself, you know!

TERRY: Yon outside t'bus wan't so far off t'mark, barmy or not. Might only be getting hundred an' eighty a week, but I fucking well work for it. I were worth a dozen o' thee this afternoon an' I got taken off.

LEE: Complain to Graham then! His decision!

TERRY: Not worth it! You say yourself he doen't know his arse from his elbow. There's me playing in t'reserves half o' t'time, and probably will be again once Noel gets his plaster off, not knowing if I'll have a job or not next season. And a clapped-out golden oldie like thee has a regular place!

LEE: Eh! Not talking to your little lottery girl now!

TERRY: She is not a fucking lottery girl! Anyway, best talk to her like that than live together an' say nowt like thee.

LEE: You've got a lot to learn, sunshine.

TERRY: Plenty o' time to do it then, haven't I? Some consolation. At least it's all in front of me.

NOEL: Look, pack it in! Both of you! Acting like bloody schoolgirls! Not going to change anything, arguing.

TERRY: He started it, talking about mi dad.

NOEL: I don't care who started it! Who bottled it, who didn't. It's over. We were a goal up, we made a mistake . . .

TERRY: He made a mistake, you mean!

NOEL: We made a mistake and we got punished. End of fucking story! Got to forget about it. Think forward to Wednesday now and make sure we stuff 'em in the replay. And you should know better, Lee! Winding him up like that!

LEE: Oh, it's my fault, is it? Regular little police constable aren't we, all of a sudden?

NOEL: You're as bad as each other. You know as well as I do: you leave it in the changing room. You get your collar and tie on and you forget it! Graham's job on Monday morning to lay blame or not. Not ours. Just cool down a bit! (*Looks out of window.*) There's Des and Graham here, anyway. Don't start sounding off again!

(*Enter* DES *in suit and tie.*)

DES: Anybody missing?

NOEL: Don't think so, Des.

DES: All got your partners, boys and girls? Yes? All right, Arthur!

(*Sound of coach moving off.* DES *gets a snack and sits next to* TERRY.)

(*To* TERRY) You look how I feel. Is there any music, Arthur?

NOEL: Rare honour, Des.

DES: Thought I'd slum it. Boost the troops' morale.

(*A Christopher Cross album starts to play softly in the background.*)

's better! (*Beat.*) I promised the wife I'd get tickets for that Chris Cross concert next month. Suppose I'd better. Keep her quiet. (*Beat.*) Cheer up, Terry! It's me got my silver wedding coming up, not you. Here – have a drink! (*Opens* TERRY*'s lager.*) Celebrate your goal. Don't see many like that these days. I told you they wouldn't be expecting you to run in from deep positions. Wouldn't have minded scoring that yourself would you, Lee?

LEE: No. No, it was a blinder, all right.

DES: What did your dad say?

TERRY: Thought it were all right.

DES: 'All right'! Should think he'll be over the moon about that. How's your eye?

TERRY: 's all right.

DES: That's all right, too, is it? Let's have a look. It'll go down. (*To* LEE) It's your foot I'm worried about.

LEE: Not exactly creaming in my pants about it myself.

DES: He's taking you to that chap in Harley Street who looked at it last time.

LEE: Who is?

DES: Graham.

LEE: What's he taking me for?

DES: I don't know.

LEE: He's never taken me before.

DES: He's taking you this time.

LEE: What for?

DES: I tell you, I don't know! Just mentioned it when we came out of the tea room.

LEE: It's not his job to take players to see specialists.

DES: He's the manager, isn't he? Can do what he likes.

NOEL: Is he going to complain about that ref?

DES: No. Too many other things on his plate. Concentrate on this replay. Have to rearrange that Southampton game now, blood and snot! Got enough fixture pile-up as it is after last winter without going in for cup draws. And Ipswich next Saturday – got to beat them if we're gonna keep up a European pressure. Forest the Tuesday after. It's all coming at the wrong time.

LEE: It's England for you, innit? Surprised they don't invent a few more cups so we can go on playing through the summer as well.

DES: There's nothing wrong with the system! Time, is it, anyway? (*Looks at watch.*) Roll on bleeding nine o'clock! (DES *stretches out. Lights fade to darkness.*)

Dim light.

Noise of coach going down motorway, and flashes of light from oncoming vehicles. Terry's seat is empty, except for his jacket. Empty beer cans, etc. on the tables.

LEE *plays patience by himself;* NOEL *dozes;* DES *is fast asleep.*

NOEL: (*Waking up suddenly*) I dreamt they took the plaster off and I had arms like the ET! Ugh! (*Looks out.*) Aren't we there yet?

LEE: Nah. Another hour yet.

NOEL: Where's Terry?

LEE: Up at the front. Talking to Graham.

NOEL: What does he want?

LEE: Dunno. Came down for him about twenty minutes ago. Still up there.

NOEL: Huh! (*Beat.*) What you playing?

LEE: Fours.

NOEL: Got it out yet?

LEE: Not yet, nah.
(*Pause.*)

NOEL: Not still thinking about the game, are you?

LEE: No! Pushed it right to the back of my mind, little thing like that.

NOEL: You should forget it, Lee.
LEE: Easy said.
NOEL: Nothing you can do about it.
(*Pause.*)
LEE: I meant to miss it, you know.
NOEL: You what?
LEE: That goal. I meant to miss it.
NOEL: Today? Piss off! Are you being serious?
LEE: It was too risky.
NOEL: You had a wide-open goal!
LEE: I know. A kid could have knocked it in. Just seemed safer to make a complete bollocks of it, all of a sudden. Scared of striking it on target in case I missed.
NOEL: But you did miss!
LEE: Well – it's what I was trying to do. It's something.
NOEL: You want to nip that one in the bud. Sharpish!
LEE: I did it at Spurs the other week.
NOEL: Have you talked to anyone?
LEE: No point. Bloke's unsure about his future, he starts creating certainties of his own. If it means missing goals . . .
NOEL: It's not your foot, is it?
(LEE *shakes his head.*)
I should have a word with someone, Lee.
LEE: There's only me can get out of it. That's all they tell you anyway at the end of the day . . . No, it's not the foot. Funny, isn't it, how you take it for granted you'll be straight down Harley Street when you get an injury like that? And the club pays. There's some geezer in Berkhamsted's promised to give me a new car if I score at Wembley next month. I already got three. I can't go into Graham's office these days without that secretary trying to get her hand inside my trousers. She treats everyone else like shit. But I'm Lee Merter. You can be a moron, you can be covered in warts, you can fart when you shake hands with the Queen at a cup final . . . as long as you're playing well . . . like being a bleeding film star.
NOEL: So?
LEE: So I don't want it to end! I like it! I like doing promotions for insurance companies, and people asking me what I think of the SDP.

NOEL: Nature of the game, isn't it? You have to plan for it.

LEE: I'm only thirty-fucking-one, Noel! I shouldn't have to plan for it! I should have it all to come ! Any other job, I would have. You go out there every Saturday for fifteen years and you perform. Excitement, adrenalin . . . They talk about the money and the glamour but it's not that. They don't mean a thing without the game. It's like you're playing for your life sometimes. Then one day they take it away from you. Like dying . . . Dying must feel like that.

NOEL: Oh, come on!

LEE: You know what President Kennedy said that time? 'You only go round the track once.' Then it's over. We haven't even done that, Noel! We've done hundred-metre fucking sprint and we're finished!

NOEL: You've just had a bad game, Lee. That's all. Happens to all of us now and again. It's not the end of the world.

LEE: Then why's he coming with me on Monday to see the specialist?

NOEL: Perhaps wants to . . .

LEE: Yeah?

NOEL: Wants to show he takes a personal interest in it. Not just leave it to Des all the time.

LEE: Do us a favour! He wants to know how long I got left before he sends me down the knacker's yard. Out to seed at somewhere like Millwall or Palace. (*Beat.*) Cold Blow Lane is where Millwall play. The Den. See it, can't you? Man in old anorak leaving by a side exit, out into Cold Blow Lane.

NOEL: I thought Barcelona was after you?

LEE: Are they, fuck! It's Bruges who are after me. FC Bruges.

NOEL: Well, you gonna go?

LEE: Have to talk to Eric on Monday – see if they've come up with anything. Might as well, I suppose. Play out my last days in the Low Countries.

NOEL: Oh, bollocks, Lee! Making me feel ill!

LEE: Yeah, well, it'll be your turn next. No good sweeping it under the carpet.

NOEL: I'm not trying to.

LEE: Oh, yeah, I was forgetting. You're joining Dock Green Police Station, aren't you?

NOEL: Knock it off! (*Beat.*) I'm under no illusions any more. Specially after today. No way I'm gonna be a Bobby

Charlton now, I know. You don't get your first England cap at my age, unless it's against Cyprus or somebody: consolation one for services to the game. Just have to accept it. I've done well to get this far really, I suppose. Not every player stays in the First Division from start to finish.

LEE: Don't start getting previous! Career's not over yet!

NOEL: That's right. I've got another six or seven years yet. At least. Drop back to a more defensive position maybe in a couple o' years time. Slow things down a bit. No reason why I shouldn't go on playing at this level though, provided I plan it right. And then . . . make sure I've got something else lined up. I'll have had a good run. (*Beat.*) What time is it?

LEE: (*Looks out of window.*) Junction 15. Should be about quarter to eight. (*Looks at watch.*) There you are! Twenty to. Know these motorways like the back of my hand. Five minutes, Newport Pagnell. Ninety minutes, the wife. (*Beat.*) I wonder what Wilma's doing?

NOEL: You didn't indulge last night, did you?

LEE: I couldn't get rid of Terry. She kept ringing up, asking if the coast was clear . . . Pity, cos I won't be due for any till I get that sauna cabin door painted. (*Beat.*) I sometimes have this dream, that instead of stopping in London, the coach keeps on going straight through. Takes us down into Kent somewhere, or across to France, and we all stay together in a nice little hotel. Quiet. Training and getting ready for the next match. And the same again after that one. Maybe spend a couple o' weeks in the close season at home. But apart from that, keep with the team.

NOEL: Go crackers!

LEE: Dunno. Could go on forever like that. Anyway, what's the alternative? 'Did you win?' 'Yeah.' 'Hungry?' 'Not really.' 'Some pie in the fridge.' Noise of her heels on the quarry tiles. Watch *Match of the Day* on my own. Fall asleep in the midnight movie . . . You haven't been over since we had that new kitchen put in, have you?

NOEL: Don't think we have, no.

LEE: You should come across some time. They get on all right, don't they? Paula an' Steph?

NOEL: Oh, yeah.

LEE: Make a day of it. We got the pool, the games room . . .

NOEL: Have to be in the next couple o' weeks. Soon as I get this plaster off I'll be up at the house in all the spare time I got.
LEE: You're on to a good wheeze there, ain't you? Having that house to escape to.
NOEL: They come with me as often as not.
LEE: No, really?
NOEL: Provided I ain't got a big job on. She helps me with bits and pieces. Kids muck around with the bricks and what have you. She's quite useful, Paula.
LEE: Course Steph keeps her hand in with her old beautician work. Still does a few friends. We had one of the rooms converted into a salon.
NOEL: It's big enough, though, isn't it, your place?
LEE: Oh, yeah, it's big enough. I sometimes go out and stand by the pool in the middle of the night when they're all asleep. Looks funny when it's all black.
NOEL: You got the dog as well.
LEE: Yes. He's a great solace is the dog.
NOEL: Must keep you occupied.
LEE: I was forgetting about him for a minute. I wonder if she took him round to Don's to have a look at that ear? Bet she didn't!
(*Sound of coach slowing down.*)
DES: (*Waking up*) We stopping?
NOEL: Looks like it, Des.
DES: Where are we?
LEE: Newport Pagnell.
DES: Must want to stretch his legs. Blood and snot! Sleeping on buses! Wonder you wake up at all sometimes. (*Sees empty seat.*) Where's Terry got to?
NOEL: He's up talking to Graham.
DES: Hmm! Unusual. Want to have a word with him. Been thinking about a new set piece to try in the replay. Him an' Lloyd linking up outside the box . . . You two getting off, then?
NOEL: Yeah, I'll come with you, Des. Shake hands with my best friend.
DES: Lee?
LEE: (*Who has been glancing at something out of the window*) Er, not for me, Des.
DES: Something wrong?

LEE: What? No. You know – the foot. You go ahead, though.

DES: Do you good to exercise it.

LEE: No, you're all right.

DES: It'd be better if . . .

LEE: I'm not getting off the coach!

DES: All right! Calm down! No good sitting around feeling sorry for yourself, you know! That's not why we pay you all that money.

LEE: Don't you start on about earning my money!

DES: It's getting fit you should be thinking . . .

LEE: I'm staying on board! All right?

DES: You are if you can pull your weight! One here (*Pointing to himself*) gonna make sure of that for a start! (*Beat, as he gets up.*) You want anything, anyway?

LEE: No, I'm fine.

DES: You coming then, Noel?

NOEL: (*Getting up*) Yeah, I'll be right with you . . .

DES: (*To* LEE) Just snap out of it!

(*Exit* DES.)

NOEL: You sure you don't want anything?

LEE: You can get us a Marathon if they have any. I like Marathons.

NOEL: Right, I'll . . .

LEE: Here, Noel! Don't forget, will you?

NOEL: About what?

LEE: Coming round sometime.

NOEL: Er, no . . . I'll have a word with Paula.

LEE: Give me a ring. Before you get the plaster off.

NOEL: I'm coming back in a minute!

LEE: Only it'll be our last chance to get together if I go . . . you know . . . to . . . abroad, like.

NOEL: Course, yeah. All right, Lee. I won't forget.

LEE: All right?

NOEL: I said, didn't I?

(*They look at each other in silence, then* NOEL *exits. Sounds off of fans singing 'There's only one team in London' to the tune of 'Guantanamera'.* LEE *flinches. Re-enter* TERRY *to get his jacket.*)

LEE: All right, Terry?

TERRY: Not bad.

LEE: Stretching your legs?

TERRY: Everybody else seems to be.
LEE: Sounds like a few of our lads out there.
TERRY: You not getting off?
LEE: Don't want 'em clamouring round you when you've got a bad foot. Always some joker who'll stand on it. (*Beat.*) Look, sorry about back there. I was all wound up myself I suppose . . .
TERRY: Yeah, yeah . . .
LEE: I should apologize. Unforgivable really – older player an' all that.
TERRY: 's all right. Forget it.
LEE: Has he given you the nod, then?
TERRY: We been talking about wine most o' t'time.
LEE: Wine?
TERRY: Home-made wine. Him an' our old feller, both mad on it. Telling me about some wheat and potato he's been making.
LEE: Oh. Thought he might have been letting you in on his plans. You know, up there in the holy of holies. Didn't he say anything about next year?
TERRY: Not a lot, no. Said he wants to see more commitment from everybody.
LEE: Well, only natural.
TERRY: Better striking force.
LEE: You put in a good word for me, then?
TERRY: Oh, aye! Asked him to give me a free transfer while I were at it. If I could a put a word in for anyone, it'd a been for missen.
LEE: Oh, sure! Understandable. You got ambition.
TERRY: He says there's a place going. I'm going to fight for it. Fucked if I'm sitting on t'subs' bench for another year.
LEE: Well, healthy way to look at it. Hope it turns out all right. (*Beat.*) Always join Noel in the police force if you don't make it. They got a good soccer team, you know.
TERRY: You think I'm stupid, don't you?
LEE: Come on, Terry! I'm only joking!
TERRY: You do! You think I'm a gormless wally from up north, I know!
LEE: I don't!
TERRY: Not much, you don't! Been laughing at me all weekend.
LEE: I haven't, Terry! You're imagining it!

TERRY: I can't be all that stupid if he asks me up front, can I? Anyway, if you want to see me like that . . . (*Starts to go.*)

LEE: I don't want to see you like that, Terry . . .
(TERRY *turns round.*)
I just can't help it!

TERRY: See! You can't leave it alone, can you?

LEE: No, no! You're taking it the wrong way!

TERRY: Aye, well, it's you should be thinking about joining t'coppers, not me.

LEE: Why? What did he say?

TERRY: He didn't say owt.

LEE: He said something. Must have done!

TERRY: He didn't have to, did he?

LEE: What's he hatching?

TERRY: Not hatching owt. He talked about planning for t'future, that's all.

LEE: And?

TERRY: That's all he said. It were just general. He didn't mention any names. You, me, nobody.

LEE: But we all know what he means, eh?

TERRY: Well, wouldn't exactly be a bolt from the blue, would it, at your age, if you got dropped? (*Beat.*) You got plans, haven't you? Not gonna be stuck for a job. Wan't you gonna start a company or somat? Or write a book?

LEE: Yeah. And I'll give you a mention. In my 'names to watch out for' chapter. The new breed who'll change nothing. Can't have England getting a name for imagination, can we?

TERRY: Tha wain't stop me, Lee. Nowt you nor any bugger else says'll stop me. I'm gonna be up there. You watch!
(TERRY *goes.*)

LEE: No, wait, Terry!
(*Exit* TERRY. *Noise off of fans greeting him. More singing off of 'There's only one team in London':* LEE *listens, then joins in, quietly at first, then with increasing volume and defiance as he changes the words.*)
(*Sings*) One team in London
There's only one team in London
One team in London
There's only one team in London.

One Lee Merter
There's only one Lee Merter
One Lee Merter
There's only one Lee Merter.

One Lee Merter
There's only one Lee Merter
One Lee Merter
There's only one Lee Merter.

ONE LEE MERTER!

(*Hold* LEE *for a few seconds in an attitude of defiance, then blackout.*)